ANGELO

A SECOND CHANCE NAVY SEAL ROMANCE

LISA CARLISLE

LISA CARLISLE

JOIN MY VIP READERS LIST!

Don't miss any new releases, giveaways, specials, or freebies! Access EXCLUSIVE bonus content.

Join the VIP list and download *Antonio: A Second Chance Marine Romance* for free today!

ALSO BY LISA CARLISLE

Anchor Me

Meet the DeMarchis brothers and their family in these romances featuring Navy SEALs or Marines!

- *Antonio (a novella available for free for subscribers. Sign up at lisacarlislebooks.com)*
- *Angelo*
- *Vince*
- *Matty*
- *Jack*
- *Slade*
- *Mark*

Night Eagle Operations

Military romantic suspense with a supernatural twist

When Darkness Whispers

Salem Supernaturals, Underground Encounters, and the White Mountain Shifters, are connected series. You can start with any of them and do not have to read in any order.

Salem Supernaturals

A witch without magic inherits a house with quirky roommates, and magical sparks fly!

- *Rebel Spell*
- *Hot in Witch City*
- *Dancing with My Elf*

White Mountain Shifters (Howls Romance)

Fated mates and forbidden love. When wolf shifters find their fated mate, the trouble is only just beginning.

- *The Reluctant Wolf and His Fated Mate*
- *The Wolf and His Forbidden Witch*
- *The Alpha and His Enemy Wolf*

Underground Encounters

Steamy paranormal romances set in an underground goth club that attracts vampires, witches, shifters, and gargoyles.

- *Book 0: CURSED (a gargoyle shifter story)*
- *Book 1: SMOLDER (a vampire / firefighter romance)*
- *Book 2: FIRE (a witch / firefighter romance)*
- *Book 3: IGNITE (a feline shifter / rock star romance)*
- *Book 4: BURN (a vampire / shapeshifter rock romance)*
- *Book 5: HEAT (a gargoyle shifter romance)*
- *Book 6: BLAZE (a gargoyle shifter rockstar romance)*
- *Book 7: COMBUST (vampire / witch romances)*
- *Book 8: INFLAME (a gargoyle shifter / witch romance)*
- *Book 9: TORCH (a gargoyle shifter / werewolf romance*
- *Book 10: SCORCH (an incubus vs succubus demon romance)*

Chateau Seductions

An art colony on a remote New England island lures creative types—and supernatural characters. Steamy paranormal romances.

- *Darkness Rising*
- *Dark Velvet*
- *Dark Muse*
- *Dark Stranger*
- *Dark Pursuit*

Highland Gargoyle

Gargoyle shifters, wolf shifters, and tree witches have divided the Isle of Stone after a great battle 25 years ago. One risk changes it all...

- *Knights of Stone: Mason*
- *Knights of Stone: Lachlan*
- *Knights of Stone: Bryce*
- *Seth: a wolf shifter romance in the series*
- *Knights of Stone: Calum*
- *Knights of Stone: Gavin (coming soon)*

Stone Sentries

Meet your perfect match the night of the super moon — or your perfect match for the night. A cop teams up with a gargoyle shifter when demons attack Boston.

- *Tempted by the Gargoyle*
- *Enticed by the Gargoyle*
- *Captivated by the Gargoyle*

Berkano Vampires

A shared author world with dystopian paranormal romances.

- *Immortal Resistance*

Blood Courtesans

A shared author world with the vampire blood courtesans.

- *Pursued: Mia*

Visit LisaCarlisleBooks.com to learn more!

ANGELO

A Navy SEAL on leave. A neuroscientist in danger.

Can one dance lead to a second chance at love?

Catherine: A stranger has been warning me about my research for the government. My coworkers tell me not to worry, but it bothers me. I can't let it show, though. This is my first time as a project lead. At least, a weekend wedding in Newport promises a much needed escape.

But when I come face to face with Angelo DeMarchis, that illusion shatters.

He's the one who got away.

And he's grown even sexier after all these years.

That's when I realize I'm in even more trouble.

And once again, the price might be my heart.

Angelo: I've needed this leave for a long time, but the memories haunt me no matter where I go.

Even at a wedding--a happy occasion--where I run into a woman from my past.

Catherine has become even hotter since high school. I wouldn't mind spending every minute I'm home with her.

There's only one problem.

Her research has gotten her into trouble.

She downplays the warnings, but I'm not buying it.

I have ten days to make sure she's safe.

She's mine and I won't let anyone get to her.

This time I'm playing for keeps.

Meet the DeMarchis family in this series by USA Today bestselling author Lisa Carlisle. Navy SEALs, Marines, and hometown heroes -- each who encounters his most complicated mission yet when a woman from his past challenges his plans for his future.

Angelo: A Second Chance Navy SEAL Romance

Copyright 2020 Lisa Carlisle

Edited by Mellow Wood Editing

Cover by Talia's Book Covers

The right of Lisa Carlisle to be identified as author of this Work has been asserted by her in accordance with sections 77 and 78 of the Copyright, Designs and Patents Act 1988.

All rights reserved. No part of this publication may be reproduced, stored in retrieval system, copied in any form or by any means, electronic, mechanical, photocopying, recording or otherwise transmitted without written permission from the publisher. You must not circulate this book in any format.

This book is licensed for your personal enjoyment only. This ebook may not be resold or given away to other people. If you would like to share this book with another person, please do so through your retailer's "lend" function. If you're reading this book and did not purchase it, or it was not purchased for your use only, then please return it and purchase your own copy. Thank you for respecting the hard work of this author.

To obtain permission to excerpt portions of the text, please contact the author at lisacarlislebooks@gmail.com.

All characters in this book are fiction and figments of the author's imagination. Any resemblance to actual events or locales or persons, living or dead, is entirely coincidental.

Find out more about the author and upcoming books online at lisacarlislebooks.com, facebook.com/lisacarlisleauthor, or @lisacbooks.

❦ Created with Vellum

CHAPTER ONE

ANGELO

*A*irports—full of happy reunions or tear-filled goodbyes. At least this time, Angelo was coming and not going. He scanned the crowd in the Providence airport looking for his family. As he searched for a familiar face, someone grabbed him from behind.

"Hey, Doc!"

Instinct drove Angelo to lift his attacker off the ground and subdue him before he registered the voice and the nickname. Dropping him back to his feet, Angelo peered into the grinning face of his youngest brother. Matty's hair was longer and his beard had grown in. He wore a Red Sox World Series T-shirt and workout shorts as he often did year-round, claiming he ran hot. And he still had the amused glimmer in his eye as if conjuring his next prank.

"I almost flipped you, dumbass. You know better than to grab someone from behind like that." Angelo pulled Matty into a bear hug.

Despite his admonition, a familiar warmth spread throughout Angelo. He'd been counting down the days for this leave for a long time, the first time he and his brothers were all together in two years. Military missions didn't plan around holidays or family events.

When he pulled back, Matty's lopsided grin spread even wider. "You should have sensed me coming." He bounced on light feet like a boxer. "Just trying to keep you on your toes."

Matty gave off the energetic vibe of a young SEAL unable to stay still, gung-ho for his next mission. Before the toll of multiple missions wore on him, before he lost his teammates, before survivor's guilt hung behind him like a weighted shadow.

"You mean attracting the attention of airport security?" Angelo groaned. "Just the way I want to start R&R."

"Being on leave doesn't mean you get to be all soft." Matty reached out to poke him in the ribs, but Angelo swatted his arm away.

"The only thing soft around here is your brain," Angelo teased. "And you're bouncing around with all the energy of the puppies you train."

"Ha, good one, Doc." Matty propped his elbow on Angelo's shoulder, the way he often did to point out that he was the tallest of the three brothers.

"Still calling me that?" Angelo was a corpsman, not a doctor, but Matty loved nicknames, even if they didn't fit.

"Of course. You're stuck with it." Matty pulled his arm away. "Come on, let's find Vince. I have a *special* way to greet him."

They grabbed their packs and maneuvered through the crowd. A couple in their fifties darted in front of them. The woman shouted "David" and waved to a teenage boy. She then embraced him like she hadn't seen him in months. The boy hugged her back, but then looked around with a sheepish expression of a teenager worried about what others thought.

"Probably away from home for the first time," Angelo noted.

He'd shed that self-consciousness at around the same age as that boy, when he'd entered the Navy and had swallowed a giant dose of humility. People didn't give a damn about you half as much as one thought. They were much more concerned with themselves. And in the ten years since, he'd seen and experienced more than he could have anticipated when he was a wide-eyed youth dreaming of military life.

Now he was at a crossroads. His tour ended next year, and he needed to decide whether to reup. Donovan's death had rattled Angelo so much that he questioned his future. But what else could he do? The Navy was the only career he'd known. He sucked in a breath. On the exhale, he rolled his shoulders and neck, trying to shake off the tension that coiled into a tight knot at the back of his neck. This wasn't the time to brood, but to celebrate a long-awaited family reunion.

A man with a high-and-tight haircut and clean-shaven face stepped through a break in foot traffic.

"Is that Vince?" Angelo walked over to get a closer look.

"Ramrod straight, like he has a stick up his ass? Game of Thrones T-shirt. Yup, that's Vince." Matty bent down and pulled a cardboard sign out from his pack. He raised it high overhead.

Mike Hawk

Welcome back from prison!

The sheep have been lonely.

Angelo chuckled. "He's going to kill you." Typical Matty humor. Vince, the most private of the brothers, would cringe at the attention.

Vince's eyes widened as he read the sign. He shook his head as he walked over.

"Hey, brother," Matty quoted Buster in *Arrested Development*, in the way he often greeted Vince.

Vince grabbed the sign and turned it upside-down, but grinned. "You're such an ass."

Matty bowed. "I try."

"And succeed," Vince added in a sardonic tone.

Angelo grinned at Vince's subdued humor. The most introverted and focused of the three of them, his ability to dig deep into his projects gave him keen insight into what made things tick. He was sharp as a scalpel when it came to machines—with people, not so much.

"Typical Matty," Angelo said. "I almost tossed him when he grabbed me from behind."

Vince raised his chin in acknowledgment and then nodded at Matty. "You finally grew in that scruff you had last Christmas."

Angelo's gut tightened. The reminder of his shitty Christmas returned. The gunfire, the—

"It's true." Matty pounded his chest. "I am all that is man!"

"Jackass." Vince laughed and then gave both his brothers a hug.

Minutes later, Angelo spotted their parents, his mother with not a strand of her dark hair out of place and his father wearing his Navy ship's baseball cap. With the way they gestured with their hands, they appeared to be bickering, how they often communicated. He smiled to himself. Was that how all couples communicated after thirty years of marriage? Not something he planned on finding out any time soon.

"Ma," Matty called out.

She turned at his voice. "There you are!" She rushed over with a jubilant smile and bear-hugged them each. "We were wondering if we had the right times and meet up spot."

His father gave them each a more reserved welcome with a quick hug and pat on the back.

When his mother started a new round of embraces, his father barked, "Come on, come on. Save it for the house, Marissa. Rush hour is about to start."

Angelo exchanged a glance with Vince and Matty. His father often attempted to outwit traffic with timing and back routes.

They squeezed into their father's gray SUV and drove south to Newport. Near the sea. Finally out of the desert. Angelo exhaled. He needed this break more than he'd realized.

That feeling continued through the evening when they gathered in the dining room of his parents' house near the Newport War College. He inhaled the scent of his mother's lasagna. It had been eons since he'd had a hearty, home-cooked meal. He would definitely enjoy the comforts of home while he could.

"It's been so long since we ate dinner together." His mother's voice caught as she scooped large slices of lasagna oozing with cheese and sauce onto the plates.

"We would have all been here last Christmas if Doc had cooperated." Matty nudged Angelo's upper arm.

"Not my decision." Damn deployment. What a shitty holiday that had been. The only lights he'd seen that night were from weapons fired.

Not now. Shelve it.

"You've got us for over a week, Ma," Matty said. "You sure you can put up with all this testosterone for that long?"

"Don't jinx it." His mother touched her silver heart necklace, a gift from their father before he went out to sea decades ago. "I know how this works."

True. An order could change everything as quick as a rifle shot.

"Smells so good!" Matty grabbed a piece of garlic bread before passing the basket.

"Much better than an MRE," Vince added.

"Eat," she commanded. "You've all gotten so thin."

Thin was a stretch. Angelo glanced at his younger brothers. All their baby fat had been trained off, replaced by muscle. He took a bite of the lasagna. The spicy rich sauce and cheese melted in his mouth, he moaned. "I don't mind putting on ten pounds if you cook like this while we're home."

"Good, your father picked up cannoli for dessert," she replied.

His dad filled their wine glasses. "Made this myself."

"You're making wine now, Pop?" Matty asked and took a sip. "Not bad. Must be nice being retired."

"I'm getting used to it. Your mother insisted I find hobbies, so I don't drive her crazy."

"Otherwise, he tells me the weather and traffic reports while I'm trying to get ready for work." She waved her hand. "Why would I care about the weather in Wyoming or the traffic in LA? I care about the traffic here, getting to work at the medical center."

His father laughed. "Who wouldn't want to know those things?" He put the wine bottle down on the table. "I've been doing more training and consulting at the base when they need me. Even lectured a few times at the War College."

"He needs some way to burn through all his restless energy," she said. "Like father—"

"Like Matty," Vince completed.

"True," Angelo agreed. Matty had inherited their dad's restlessness and often sought new projects. It could be a new sport or activity, or the latest video game. Matty had to experience everything.

"Almost a miracle to have all of you home at the same time. Ryan is thrilled you're going to make it to his wedding." His dad's voice took on a wistful edge, one Angelo had rarely heard from the no-nonsense naval captain.

"Not even the Navy could keep me from my cousin's wedding," Matty declared with a lopsided grin. Neither was true. The Navy could easily do so, and Ryan wasn't technically a cousin. They knew their dad's best friend since they were kids. They'd called him Uncle Steve, making Ryan a "cousin."

"What time is the wedding tomorrow?" Angelo asked.

"Five." His mother dished out more helpings of lasagna to anyone who had a spot cleared on their plate.

Her Italian and Armenian heritage correlated to massive amounts of delicious food when they were home. He was definitely going to put on some weight if he ate like this. He'd have to make sure he got his daily training in.

"Oh, it's beautiful there." His mother clasped her hands in delight. "A perfect Newport wedding on the ocean."

"With several hot single women, I hope." Matty raised a speculative brow.

Vince leaned back in his chair. "They'll all look like supermodels to me at this point. Been a long time."

Angelo agreed with a grunt. Far. Too. Long.

His dad sipped his wine and leaned back, staring at the glass as if analyzing his latest batch. "Anything you boys want to see or do while you're home?"

The three brothers exchanged glances. Matty answered for them. "Women."

His mom swatted him with a dish towel. "I don't want to hear about it."

"Come on, Marissa," his father teased. "You think you'd be used to it by now."

"Sad, but true." She nodded with a knowing smile. "I've heard more than my ears ever wanted to hear."

Angelo took another bite of lasagna. A woman would be a welcome distraction. One night with no-strings-attached could help release some of the tension that had wormed inside every nerve and muscle. No matter how often he stretched on a foam roller or sought mindfulness with deep breathing and visualizations, images of combat would intrude on his peace of mind like a snoring bunkmate.

Yes, one night with a beautiful woman was a good plan.

"Plenty of single women at a wedding," Matty noted in a conspiratorial tone.

Angelo raised his glass. "I've been warned countless times in the military to never volunteer. But I'll be the first to sign up for that mission."

CATHERINE

Catherine shouldn't have checked her notifications. She was in a room upstairs at the wedding venue on Saturday afternoon with the others in the bridal party. They shared champagne, shrimp cocktail, and stuffed mushrooms before heading downstairs for the wedding ceremony.

When her phone buzzed, she'd checked it out of habit. Maybe a *bad* habit. In this case, it did nothing to help her with her frayed nerves.

Trent, the man who had contacted her about her work last week, had found her on social media. She had blocked him through her work email, but he had found another way to contact her.

You haven't responded to my letters or email. I am waiting. I've warned you about your research. You must stop the project.

She shivered as if a thousand insects crawled over her skin. He'd have to keep waiting since she had no intention of answering per guidance from the security team at the university. They would handle it. Sure, a part of her felt badly for him, but that was up to a professional in a different field. Her focus was on the brain and on memory research in particular, not treating a patient who believed the government was trying to wipe his memories.

Catherine pictured her two cousins and what they'd gone through when they were kids. What they'd suffered with numerous brain surgeries had inspired her to keep going through the years of intense studying to become a neuroscientist. She wasn't going to let a stranger deter her goals.

Besides, coming here to the wedding in Newport was supposed to be a fun weekend getaway, not more work. She turned off all notifications, shoved her phone into her purse, and returned her attention to her friend, the bride.

Half an hour later, Catherine waited for her turn to walk down the aisle. Her heart beat and skin turned clammy. She dreaded the impending walk with dozens of eyes tracking her every step. Was it stage fright or was she still rattled by the intrusive contact?

Probably a little of both.

Relax, nobody is here to see you. They're waiting to see the bride and groom. If the five-year-old flower girl can handle it, don't you think you can too?

True. She inhaled the scent of roses and ocean. Her gaze followed the trail of pink rose petals on either side of the grassy path leading to a white pagoda where the groom and groomsmen waited.

Plastering on a smile, she stepped forward, focusing on the waves flowing in from the bay rather than the people staring at her. She counted her steps to steady her nerves—numbers were a surefire way to refocus. They were comforting. Which was why she loved math. It had rules. Structure. Before long she reached her destination. Pivoting past the groom, she took her designated spot opposite the groomsmen as they had practiced last night. She exhaled, the worst part was over.

The rest of the bridesmaids followed and then came Diana, wearing a beautiful, princess-like strapless dress and beaming with happiness, clearly relishing this moment. Catherine had heard many versions of her dream Newport wedding during their time rooming together at MIT. When Diana had met Ryan during trivia night at a local pub two years ago, she had no doubt her friend had found the one.

Catherine watched the two of them exchange vows and reflected on how different her path had gone from Diana's since their graduation. She didn't share those dreams of a happy ever after. Dating had taken a backseat as she pursued a Ph.D. program studying the biology of the brain. What few relationships she'd had were short term and devoid of passion. Perhaps that was for the better. Her friends had been tormented by relationships, spending countless hours analyzing some guy who was usually soon out of the picture. Now that she worked at a university in Providence, she didn't have time to waste on the nonsense surrounding relationships.

She glanced out at the wedding guests. Did she know anyone? When she spotted a man seated on the groom's side, she stifled a gasp.

Angelo DeMarchis.

It couldn't be him. No… Not here, not now…

Was it, though? She couldn't be sure from this distance and she wasn't about to stare.

How many times had she fantasized about running into him? As the years went on, she'd long since accepted a romantic reunion was *not* going to happen. She lived in Providence and he could be deployed anywhere in the world. But, now ten years after he'd enlisted, he was seated at her friend's wedding in Newport.

Whenever she'd heard news about the troops, she thought of him. Was he still in the Navy? Was he safe? She was not prepared for this. All those cute fantasies she'd had when she was younger shattered, replaced by a sweaty-palm fear. She stared at her bouquet of calla lilies and clutched them more tightly.

Calm down. You're getting worked up over nothing.

Maybe it wasn't Angelo after all. This was just a byproduct of her nerves. This guy had a beard and his dark hair was longer than the crewcut she remembered. She'd thought she'd seen him around Rhode Island countless times before only to be let down when she discovered it was a stranger.

Which option did she want—for it to be him or not?

Catherine blinked slowly before glancing at him again, ready to accept that she'd projected his face onto yet another stranger. He smiled at her and she quickly averted her gaze. The men beside him had to be his two brothers and his parents. She'd only met them a couple of times but recognized them. No doubt this was Angelo.

Damn.

Images of their last night together returned. That unforgettable night when they'd kissed—and had gotten so close to doing so much more. She'd put on the brakes and had questioned her actions countless times since.

The anxiety of walking down the aisle minutes before now seemed like a piece of that multi-tiered wedding cake. Time slowed down. She no longer heard what the justice of the peace was saying.

What would she say to him after all these years? Her body shifted into overdrive, heart pumping wildly. Should she go for a casual tone, like they were long-lost acquaintances? Or, a bit more reserved, yet not aloof. Seconds ticked by like a swinging pendulum while her mind raced over what might happen next.

For someone so analytical, who didn't just have plans, but many backup options for a multitude of scenarios, nothing came to her.

Nothing.

CHAPTER TWO

ANGELO

*A*ngelo took his seat beside his family at Ryan's wedding. The setting sun draped the sky in golds and oranges over the Narragansett Bay. He inhaled the ocean air, and the salty scent comforted him. Damn, it felt great to be here, surrounded by the sea rather than sweltering in a desert or freezing on a cold, barren night in the middle of nowhere.

Minutes later, the band played, signaling the beginning of the wedding ceremony. Angelo turned back with the other guests to face the historic estate, now a seaside retreat and popular wedding site. A flower girl walked out from behind the brick building and tossed flower petals. Following her came the bridesmaids, all wearing rose-colored dresses.

Matty nudged Angelo and whispered, "Look at the hotties."

He glanced at the handful of women lined up. A brunette looked familiar. At this distance, he wasn't sure.

Nah, he was probably imagining that once again. How many times had he thought he recognized someone during deployments? Human nature, probably. Trying to find a familiar connection in strange surroundings.

Throughout the ceremony, his gaze returned to the bridesmaid standing in front of the bay. Even at this distance, she was a vision under the setting sun. Her dark hair was pulled up with loose curly tendrils framing her face and her hair shone with a reddish hue under the sunlight. Although she wore the same rosy-pink dress as the other bridesmaids, it hugged her curves in a way that made him take a closer look. Oof, yes. She was the one.

The ceremony ended, and one of the groomsmen extended his arm for her to take a hold of. Angelo scowled. If they were together, that would kill any chance he had. He studied their body language to see if there was any sort of familiarity between them, anything to indicate they were a couple. No, they both appeared stiff, not quite comfortable with each other. A good sign.

As soon as he saw an opening, he would make his move before somebody else moved in. Like his brothers. He glanced at his watch. If the wedding party took photos after the ceremony, she wouldn't return for some time.

She didn't. Angelo kept an eye out for her during cocktail hour and once they entered the reception area for dinner. He didn't see her until he returned from the restroom. She was standing on the side of the dance floor with the rest of the bridal party as the bride and groom were introduced.

He returned to the table where his family was seated with a younger naval family who had recently relocated to Newport. While they dined on a New England style seafood dinner, complete with clam chowder, boiled lobster, steamed clams, and cornbread, his parents gave the younger family tips about the base and raising a family in Newport.

"No finer place to sail," his dad said.

"And the schools are very good," his mom added. "Several programs for the kids."

Matty nudged Angelo and Vince and nodded to the head table. "Which one of you suckers is next?"

"I didn't dodge bullets overseas only to get hit by one back at home," Vince replied in his characteristic dry tone.

"Must be you, Doc," Matty said.

Him? Angelo tried to picture himself as the groom in this setting, saying vows to his bride in front of the bay. The image was blurry, static.

"Not going to happen." He leaned back in the chair. "Doesn't fit the lifestyle."

"True," Matty said.

Vince nodded.

Throughout dinner, his mother gushed about her sons to acquaintances.

"Tell him where you've been." His mother nudged Angelo's arm after chatting with a man with graying hair.

"Ma, you know we're not supposed to talk about that."

The man chuckled. "If you tell me, you have to kill me, right?"

Angelo suppressed a groan. How many times had he heard that one?

Matty cut in, "We'd rather have a drink with you."

Angelo glanced at his youngest brother. He was most at ease in social situations, while Vince was more reserved, more fascinated by technology than people. Angelo had definitely taken on the leadership role, feeling a responsibility to take care of them. That mindset had carried over to the SEALs where he took care of others as their corpsman.

"You're all active duty now?" The man asked. "Impressive."

"Yep, we followed our dad into the Navy," Matty said.

"Marines," Vince clarified.

"You know the Marines fall under the Department of the Navy," Matty said, repeating their often-resurrected debate.

"That doesn't make me a sailor."

"That doesn't make you a SEAL, either."

Angelo laughed. Branch rivalry. Sibling rivalry. They'd never run out of fodder.

Matty turned to his father's friend. "Angelo is a corpsman and Vince is an EOD tech."

"And Matty works with puppies," Vince teased, before taking a swig of beer.

"K9s," Matty clarified. "And they've saved many of our asses out there."

"True," Angelo agreed. A recent close call with an IED had been detected by a K9. Too close. But there were the other times where his team wasn't as lucky. He shuddered as a hot flash swept through him.

One memory seeped in. A situation that turned devastating in a flash. The lights, the gunfire, the smell of combat. His heart pounded, and skin flushed from the memories. He gritted his teeth, forcing away sounds of explosives and visions of blood.

No, not now. He couldn't let the dark thoughts creep in now. He left the table to get some fresh air. A sliver of the moon and the first few stars twinkled in the darkening sky. He gulped in the sea air. *Snap out of it. You're home.* He attempted to breathe through it, but the band playing "'Til There was You" echoed in his ears.

Angelo strolled from the venue, needing to clear his head before he rejoined the ceremony. He followed the four-count breathing technique he learned in the SEALs to stay calm under stressful situations *Breathe in through the nose for four seconds, hold for four, exhale for four, hold for four.*

He spent a few minutes strolling on the grass away from the venue. The music grew more faint as the calming sound of the ocean wrapped around him. When he felt ready to return to the celebration, the notes of Frank Sinatra's "The Way You Look Tonight" grew louder.

There she was. Alone.

The bridesmaid stood outside the reception hall, staring at her phone. The light from it gave her location away in the shadows.

This was his chance to talk to her. He strode over to her. A moment's hesitation could cost him, just like it could on the battlefield.

"Great wedding, isn't it?"

She glanced at him for a flash before avoiding his gaze and muttering, "Yes."

Shit. Maybe this was a bad idea. Not only did she not seem interested, his uncomfortable memories lingered like perspiration after a run.

Once again, he was struck by how familiar she looked. Asking *'Don't I know you from somewhere?'* would sound so cheesy that he might as well join the platter of goat cheese and cheddar that were served as appetizers.

He glanced inside. Couples were dancing. Yes, that was it. A dance. He wasn't ready to give up yet.

"Would you like to dance?"

Silence ticked like a grenade. Why had he barked out that invitation without even introducing himself? Damn, those memories had rattled him, killing any attempt at being smooth. He wouldn't blame her if she shot him down like he was hit by an RPG. What a rock.

"Sure." She smiled and stashed her phone into her purse.

He exhaled. He hadn't blown it after all. They entered the reception area. The lights had dimmed to a softer, more romantic glow. She stashed her purse beneath a table. Not a very good strategy to keep thieves from snatching it, but he'd keep an eye out on her behalf. Maybe he was being overcautious and should just force himself to enjoy the moment.

He offered her a hand. When she took it, a sizzling sensation rippled through him. Why? He couldn't identify why it affected him and that was unnerving.

The song ended. Shit, if a fast one followed, he'd have to make a quick exit. He wouldn't be the awkward, ambling guy making an ass out of himself.

A slow Shania Twain song played. Nice, he could work with this. He led them onto the dance floor and wrapped his free hand around her waist, moving them into the dance. A light floral scent tickled his nostrils, not overpoweringly heavy like how some women doused themselves, but enough to tempt him to inhale more deeply. He kept his urge in check.

Other parts of his body had different urges in mind, ones more difficult to ignore. She felt so good in his arms. If holding her in a dance felt this good, having her in bed would be incredible. He fantasized how that would play out. Before he got an erection, he searched for something else to divert his attention.

Combat. No. Hell no. Images had already paralyzed him enough tonight.

You're holding a beautiful woman in your arms, the one you've had your eye on all night. Don't blow it.

He exhaled, staring out the open door to the ocean to force the remaining tension out of his limbs. "I'm Angelo. Friend of the groom's family. What's your name?"

She faltered, and he held her closer to break her fall.

"Whoa, heels and a dress. Never understood how women could walk in them."

CATHERINE

Angelo didn't recognize her? What. The. Hell?

Catherine's mind swarmed with racing thoughts as she tried not to let it show how he'd affected her. She kept her eyes averted, focusing on other couples dancing around them or the band exacerbating her torment by repeating, "You're still the one."

She focused on moving her body along as he led them in this dance, while trying to ignore the heat zinging through her body.

The night had morphed from semi-awkward to utter shit. First, Trent had contacted her on social media. And then—Angelo. Emotions roiled through her as the past crashed with the present. After he'd first pulled her close, she'd barely been able to breathe with having him so near, the heat from his body doing strange things as it warmed her. At least, she could keep from meeting his gaze while they danced. In this closed space, his proximity would be too intense.

Still, she'd glimpsed enough to note he'd grown from a teenage boy into a man—a man who filled out every line and angle of his suit to mouthwatering perfection. The beard suited him, adding to the devastating allure.

When he'd extended his hand to dance, she'd curled her fingers around his. The mere touch of his skin sent sparks dancing up her arm. A flush rose in her chest, and she prayed it didn't reach her face. She was not a blushing teenager any longer; she was an educated woman with a career. She should not let a simple dance rattle her.

But there was nothing simple about it. When he'd clasped one hand and dropped his other to her lower back, she could barely remember how to dance. With her breaths turning shallow, she'd had to take a deep inhale to regain enough oxygen. She'd momentarily forgotten where to put her other hand until he led. Luckily, her hand seemed to know where to find his shoulder.

As he led her on this dance, the connection between them simmered. Heat, vibrant and powerful, radiated through her body. She couldn't let him see how he'd affected her. Hadn't she just been up here with the groomsman she was paired with minutes ago? She compared this dance to the previous one. A mandatory pairing, almost clinical. No sparks.

But with Angelo? Wow. Almost magical.

She hadn't experienced a reaction this powerful in the years they'd been apart, not since the night before he'd shipped out. In the years that followed, she thought she must have built the memory up to something greater in her mind, but now touching him, his hands on her, it all came rushing back. It was real. It had always been.

Until he just admitted he didn't know who she was. Ouch. Humiliation hit her hard, twisting inside her with a burn that intensified with each moment. Being overlooked hit one of her sore spots. The quiet, brainy ones like her were often invisible.

Catherine wasn't naïve enough to think that Angelo still held a torch for her, but maybe, just maybe a spark of interest. Since he'd asked for her name, that doused that fantasy like a flash flood. She wasn't important enough to be remembered.

With him so close, and his lips just inches from hers, he was close enough to kiss.

Or slap.

Why not? He deserved it. She'd jolt him with a reminder of *exactly* who she was. Was she so inconsequential among the women in his life that she didn't even register as someone from his past? He was the one who looked so damn different with longer hair and she'd still been able to recognize him from afar.

She focused on other couples dancing around them. Happy couples. Couples in love. Not suffering from a smoldering, mortifying burn. No way would she give him the satisfaction of knowing how his words had hurt her.

"So, what is it?" he asked, interrupting her thoughts.

"What's what?"

"Your name."

Shit, she'd gone way down memory lane, forgetting to respond. If she told him who she was and he still didn't remember her, that would be a double blow. And at a wedding no less. Total rejection. Not here, not now. Self-preservation kicked in. Swallowing a lump that had frozen in her throat, she gave the first name that came to mind. "Melody."

As soon as the name fell from his lips, a twinge of regret hit her. Maybe lying wasn't the best option.

Ah, but she'd been identified when they'd introduced the bridal party.

"Melody," he repeated. "Like a song. I like it."

She exhaled. He didn't seem to note the discrepancy. Maybe he'd been distracted.

"Are you family or friend?" he asked.

Should she continue with the lie? Keeping up with one would be hard enough, the deeper she went in, the harder it would be to remember the details. "Friend. Diana and I were roommates in college." That was true.

"And you're still close. That's great."

He pulled her a tad tighter as they danced, and she became hyperaware of how her body reacted to his touch. Good God, he smelled so good. A clean-soap scent and underlying male musk that was so alluring she could lean into his chest and drown in it. His closeness was impossible to ignore, swallowing up the space between them with magnetic power.

The lyrics swam in her head, tormenting Catherine with a reminder that she'd never truly gotten over him.

When another couple exchanged a quick greeting with Angelo, she stole a glance at his face. The years were more than just kind to him, they were unfairly gracious. He'd lost the cuteness of his teenage face as he'd filled out to a man. Gone was the youthful innocence, replaced by the experience of a man who might have seen too much. What was it that he'd gone through over the last decade? She wanted to ask him about the Navy, see if he went for his dream of becoming a SEAL. Was he still in? They'd kept in touch in the beginning, but with busy lives separating in different directions, they'd lost touch.

Ah, she couldn't ask him anything since she'd supposedly just met him moments before. She was Melody, a bridesmaid, and he was a wedding guest, Angelo, whom she knew nothing about.

Except how good her traitorous body felt being in his arms despite the mental anguish of being forgotten.

He's a jerk. Totally forgot you. You're probably just one on a long list of women in his life.

Was she overreacting? They'd never been serious. They'd lived several towns apart and neither had a car. Spring of senior year swarmed with graduation activities and they'd only gotten together a handful of times. Their short relationship was mostly over the phone. Besides, it was foolish to grow attached to someone the spring before high school graduation when he'd be going to the Navy and her to MIT.

But she had.

Their relationship clearly meant more to her than him. Humiliation resurfaced with a biting sting. She wanted to ream him out.

No, not here. She couldn't make a scene at her friend's wedding. That would make her the shittiest of bridesmaids. If she learned anything in her first time in this role, it was not to steal attention from the bride on her big day.

"Where did you and Diana go to school?" Angelo asked.

Catherine pursed her lips before replying. In their senior year, he knew she was going to MIT. In fact, she'd tried to convince him to go to college with his stellar academic record. One of their conversations about it flashed in her mind.

"Why not go to college and join ROTC?" she'd asked.

"I can go to school while in the Navy," he'd said.

He'd been hell-bent on becoming a Navy SEAL as soon as possible. What he hadn't told her was that he'd already enlisted. He'd saved that for the following week when he'd said goodbye, said he was headed out to basic training. That had been the last time she'd seen him until tonight.

Not wanting to ring any bells to trigger who she really was, she lied. "Brown." It wasn't completely a lie since she went there for her PhD, but it wasn't where she roomed with Diana.

She kept her gaze averted. What if he knew where Diana went to school? Crap, if she kept building up her tall tale, it would end up crumbling apart eventually, like a game of Jenga.

"What about you?" she asked. "How do you know Diana and Ryan?"

"Ryan's father is my dad's old Navy buddy. They're like family to us."

"Oh," she replied, wanting to follow up with many questions, but not sure where to start. "Are you in the military too?"

"Guilty. My dad's retired, but my youngest brother and I are both Navy. My other brother is a Marine."

"We're the third generation in the service," he added. "My grandfather moved here from Italy and lied about his age to enlist at seventeen."

"Committed."

Her mind raced back to the end of senior year. She'd taken his departure after graduation hard, no matter how many times she'd tried to convince herself it was stupid.

What stung most was how often she'd thought of him since then. She had debated on searching for him online, but never did. If he was happily married with a brood of kids, she didn't want it paraded around in front of her.

Now he was here at the wedding with no wedding band in sight and no sign of a girlfriend or fiancée.

Shania sang the final lines, which meant Catherine's mortification could soon end. She could run away and pretend she never ran into him here tonight.

A hollow ache expanded inside her. Why did that option torment her worse than being forgotten?

Haunted by her conflicting thoughts and the heat simmering on every spot where he touched her body, she barely noticed when the band shifted into a more upbeat song. The other bridesmaids hooted and dragged others onto the floor.

"Woo, let's dance!" Diana's cousin said, clasping her hand.

"One second." She pulled her hand away and glanced at Angelo.

"Thanks." He smiled. "Have fun with the ladies. Maybe we can have a drink later."

He walked away, and she was instantly swallowed in a sea of rose satin-clad bridesmaids. The spots of her body where his hands had been now cooled with his sudden absence. Remembering her duties, she cheered and danced with the others, while trying to process what had happened.

She glanced out through the crowd to find him, but he'd disappeared. If he asked about her at all, her tangled web of fabrications could unravel with the slightest tug. Lying might not have been the best option.

Too late now. She bit her lip. Could she get through the night without him discovering her duplicity?

CHAPTER THREE

ANGELO

After the dance, Angelo searched for his family. He spotted his brothers in a line three deep at the bar.

He smirked. "How did I guess I'd find you here?"

"Open bar. Hardly a challenge," Matty noted with a lopsided grin.

Vince gave a half-nod. "Who were you dancing with?"

"Friend of the bride." Angelo stared at each of them and warned with a lighthearted grin, "And back off."

Matty laughed. "Come on, even the K9s I work with aren't this territorial."

"Shots for all," his father announced, joining them at the bar. He placed the order and then said, "Stogies on the beach. Who's in?"

"Haven't had one of those in years," Angelo replied. Possibly not since returning from his first deployment. He'd been so green. Treating the wounded had taken more of an emotional toll than he'd anticipated. Those dark memories could wait until he was alone. No doubt they'd worm their way into his mind.

Vince handed out the shot glasses the bartender had placed on the bar. "To being together again."

"Hell yeah," Matty said. "Who knows if and when we'll get a chance to do this again?"

The unspoken loomed between them. Anything could go wrong during a mission and usually did. Not everyone returned home.

Their father raised his glass, but when he spoke his voice hitched. "To now and many more times in the future."

Angelo drank the shot. The whiskey burned down his throat. After they all lowered their glasses, they exited out the French doors onto a grassy area before the beach. A group of people smoked cigars near a cluster of white Adirondack chairs facing the bay, twinkling lights reflecting on the water's surface. The scent of cigar smoke mixed in with that of the ocean.

When Ryan saw them approach, he hugged each one and handed them cigars. "I can't believe you all made it to my wedding. My favorite uncle and cousins!"

They laughed. They'd spent more time growing up with their adopted naval families than their blood relatives.

"We're thrilled to be here," Angelo replied.

"Congrats," Vince added.

"Looks like you found yourself a good woman." Matty glanced around. "How are you already out of her sight?"

"She's catching up with old friends. Good time to escape for a cigar," Ryan said. "But you're right, I'm a lucky guy." He nodded. Glancing at each in turn he said, "None of you are ready to take the plunge yet?"

"Hell no," Matty said. "Doesn't fit with the lifestyle."

"Oh, come on," Ryan said. "Your parents have been married for what, over thirty years?" He turned to their dad for confirmation.

"Affirmative," his father said. "And I was in the Navy for most of the time."

His father had left out the times when he and his mom had separated. Military marriages were difficult. Multiple moves and deployments took a toll. Angelo couldn't put someone through what his mother had gone through.

"I'm away more than home," Angelo said. "Few women would put up with that."

Angelo had met some of his teammates' wives. They were strong, patient—it took a special woman to sign up for this lifestyle where the mission came first.

He peeked into the reception area. Melody's back was toward him as she danced with the other bridesmaids and friends. They were having a good time, the way girls did when they got together and danced, smiling about who-knows-what girl things. The sway of her body in that satin dress did fresh things to his libido. What was she like?

Wait, he'd had *one dance* with her. He wanted to spend the night with her, that was it. What the hell had gotten into him? One more example of how the last mission had rattled him, making him search for a safe anchor while he was on leave.

Pathetic.

He didn't do relationships. As the saying went, he was already married to the SEALs.

"Whoever's footing the bill is going to flip when they see the tab," Matty said. "Didn't they know how many sailors would be here tonight?"

"My dad's call, and it's on him," Ryan said. "He said sailors don't give a crap about the flower arrangements or ice sculptures, but they care a hell of a lot about the drinks."

"Your dad's a smart man and absolutely right." Matty raised his glass. "Cheers."

Angelo zeroed in on Melody again. He wanted to go back and dance with her but nope, bad idea. Slow dancing was fine, but he definitely did not have *Moves like Jagger*, the song playing, no matter what the whiskey might be telling him. His finesse moving through obstacles with a weapon didn't carry over to the dance floor.

"Damn, Doc," Matty said. "You got a hard-on for that girl or what?"

Angelo blinked before turning to his brother. "What?"

"You keep staring at her."

"Careful," Vince said. "She's going to think you're creeping on her."

Shit. They were right. He had to snap out of it.

Ryan turned to look. "Who is it?"

"No one," Angelo said.

"The bridesmaid to the left of Diana," Matty pointed out.

"Catherine?" Ryan said.

"No, Melody," Angelo clarified.

"Melody?" Ryan scrunched his face in deep thought. "I don't know any guests named Melody. Definitely not one of the bridesmaids."

Matty's eyes widened and his face contorted with amusement before he burst into laughter. "She lied to you about her name."

"Brilliant," Vince added in a wry tone. "Smooth."

"Funny." He ignored them and turned to Ryan. "The brunette in the pink bridesmaid's dress, her name is Catherine?"

Ryan nodded. "Yes. She was Diane's roommate in college."

Angelo gritted his teeth as his warning antennae went up. "At Brown, right?"

"Brown?" Ryan repeated. "No. Where did you get that?"

More snickers from his brothers followed. Melody, or Catherine whatever her real name was, had said Brown. No question about it, she'd straight up lied to him.

He swallowed hard. He detested lies. If she wasn't interested in him, fine. She didn't have to play him and make him look like an ass in front of his family and friends.

Time to confront her and find out why she lied to him. Twice.

CATHERINE

Catherine stared at herself in the mirror of the ladies' room. Did she look all that different from what she'd looked like at seventeen? Her hair was pinned up and locked in place, courtesy of countless hair products the stylists had used on her earlier. Curly tendrils hung loosely at the sides of her face, softening the pinned back look. And she'd enhance the drab brown color with a reddish hint. Maybe it wasn't what he was used to—straight brown hair that hung without a hint of a wave down her back.

What about her face? Certainly, that hadn't changed too much in ten years. Sure, she ditched her eyeglasses for contacts, and the stylists had painted her with more makeup than she ever thought she'd agree to wear, but still. It was her face!

And her voice—another thing he *could* have recognized but *didn't*. Sure, they hadn't said more than a few words. Hot tears burned her eyes. Damn him.

A reminder of his delicious scent and how she practically lit up in his arms worked its way through the anguish. No, she wouldn't think of that. She wasn't a naïve, love-struck teenager anymore. She wouldn't get sucked in by his charm again. Besides self-preservation, she could go for a little payback. Rattle him up to make him uncomfortable. But how?

She thought of some pranks her students had run. No, she didn't have the capacity to pull off anything elaborate. But, there had to be a way to make him squirm. What had made her uncomfortable?

That disturbing message from Trent was still vivid in her mind. Maybe she could work with that. As she tried to brainstorm a plan, the ladies room door flung open. Diana burst in, her cheeks aglow, appearing radiant in her white satin gown with her blonde hair and makeup still perfect. On spotting Catherine's troubled expression, Diana's smile dropped.

"Uh oh, what is it?"

"Nothing, nothing." She wiped her eyes. "I'm not used to all this mascara."

"Bull," Diana replied. "I've lived with you long enough to know when something's bothering you *and* when you're lying to me."

"Forget it," she said. "It's stupid. Besides this is your big day. Not the time to talk about my ridiculous issues."

"Come on, Catherine. I'm not a Bridezilla demanding the spotlight. You're my friend, and something's bothering you. I've only seen you tear up when it's been something big."

"That's the thing. It's not something big, it's stupid." She swallowed the lump in her throat. "And the way I'm letting it get to me bothers me even more."

Diana handed her a tissue and turned to face the mirror. "Don't worry, I'm not going to pity-stare at you the way you hate. I'll refresh my makeup while you talk. Now spill."

She took a deep breath before she gave Diana the condensed version of what had happened with Angelo.

"Ah, that sucks. But playing devil's advocate, you do look different from college." She moved loose strands of hair back into place. "Better, in fact. You've bloomed over the years."

"Thanks, but—when you know someone, you think you'd recognize other things about them."

Diana made a noncommittal sound. "So, what are you going to do?"

"I have two options. One, avoid him for the rest of the night. Two, screw with him a little. Maybe act in some way to make him uncomfortable."

"Why would you want to do that?" Diana applied a coat of lip gloss.

"You don't know how stupid I feel. You know the awkwardness when you recognize someone, but they've forgotten you?"

"Yes."

"Well, imagine that a hundred times worse. Because you've dated the guy and *thought* it meant something. But *clearly*, you were wrong. And you are forgettable."

Diana's brows furrowed. "Don't see how it's going to make you feel any better."

Catherine sighed. "Maybe you're right." Why was she getting so emotional over this? He didn't recognize her. Big deal. It was a long time ago. They were teenagers. No matter how analytically she tried to assess the situation and dismiss her irrational reaction, she couldn't shake how it hit her like a raw slap.

"How about a third option?" Diana tapped her chin before replying. "Sleep with him."

"What!"

"Why not?" Diana powdered her nose casually. "I mean you've had a thing for him. Sometimes you need to act on those urges to get them out of your system."

"You know I'm not into quick hookups."

"The best part is," Diana continued, "He doesn't know who you are. You get to be whatever woman you want to be and act out any fantasy. Harmless fun. Nobody gets hurt."

An image of bringing Angelo to her room formed in her mind, quickly shaping into rich, decadent fantasies. Maybe Diana was right, she could do things with him she'd never dreamed possible.

Pushing aside her sordid thoughts, she returned to her reality. She was an analytical scientist, not some vixen who specialized in seduction. "I don't know if I can do that."

Diana faced her and grinned. "But I can tell you're thinking about it."

Catherine blushed. Was she so transparent?

"Hey, it's your life, your decision," Diana added. "Forget about him right now. Let's dance and have a damn good time."

"I'll be out in a couple of minutes."

Diana left and Catherine touched up her makeup. Applying a fresh coat of a deep rose lipstick, something she rarely wore. Stepping back, she took an objective look at herself. She did look pretty good. The dress flattered her body shape, accentuating her breasts, which she usually hid under conservative clothing at the university. Combined with the hair and makeup, she was almost on the sexy scale. Maybe she could play the part of the seductress for this one night.

Holding her head high, she exited into the hall area, wondering if she could pull off Diana's plan and seduce Angelo. As soon as she returned to the reception area, he stepped in her path and she sucked in a breath.

"We need to talk."

The grave tone of his voice instantly set off flare warnings and put her on the defensive. All inklings of seduction vanished like vapor from the melting ice sculpture.

"Shh," she said, pressing a finger to her lips.

What was she doing? Her half-assed plan of making him sweat took over.

She darted her eyes around the room with suspicion. "You don't want them to hear us."

He stood ramrod straight and scanned every angle with scrutiny. "Who?"

Good question. Where she was going with this? Uneasiness about Trent contacting had to have crept under her skin and hovered near the forefront of her mind. She leaned closer and whispered. "The government."

He blinked rapidly before squinting at her. "Excuse me?"

"They're trying to control us." She tapped her temple for emphasis. "To control our minds."

She had to be losing her mind to put on this act. It was ridiculous. Childish. A horrible idea. But a part of her relished his obvious uneasiness after how insignificant she'd felt when they'd danced.

"You." She pointed at his chest. "You must be one of them."

"What the—?"

His shocked expression almost made her break character. Forget what Diana had dismissed about this idea, witnessing his discomfort for a few moments was worth it. Before she burst into laughter, she turned away and hurried outside.

"Wait," he called.

She didn't stop to turn back but ran outside the venue and found a private spot near an air conditioning vent. Laughter spilled out. God that felt good to see him squirm.

After the moment passed, a twinge of regret followed. Reacting this strongly wasn't like her. She took a clinical approach to her work and avoided drama in her life, yet the way she acted tonight was far from rational. She shook her head. Her only explanation was that it was Angelo, and her feelings for him had never been neutral.

Things could have gone better if she'd listened to Diana. She could have played a different role with a more satisfying physical outcome. A vision of them tangled in the luxurious sheets upstairs flashed before her.

Too late. Besides, she couldn't pull off the role of a seduction, anyway. She was too analytical and too structured to follow a lustful itch.

And one night with him could set her up in a trap where she fell for him all over again. If she'd learned anything from her experiences, which was solidified earlier tonight, it was that Angelo DeMarchis could bring her nothing but pain.

Angelo

Angelo kept his distance while he followed to the side of the building where the woman had fled. He couldn't let a disturbed woman run off from a wedding. That's all the bride wanted on her wedding day—putting together a search party for one of the bridesmaids.

Still, he had no clue as to what precipitated the change. She was nothing like the woman who had danced with him earlier, who'd felt so good in his arms, who'd smelled so damn delicious. Was she on a medication that wore off? Was that why she'd lied to him?

As he approached, her laughter reached him.

That laugh, he knew it. Knew it all so well. In a rush, it all came together. The familiarity, the odd sense of a connection. She might look different tonight in a bridesmaid's dress with her hair up and without glasses, but he'd *never* forget her laugh. He had strived many times to break through her serious nature to hear that musical sound.

Her first name was Catherine, just as Ryan had said. In high school, she went by Cate.

Cate Boudreaux. Oh yes, he remembered her. How could he forget? They'd met during a National Honor Society event during the spring of senior year. Although they lived towns apart, they grew close during the last couple of months before he went into the Navy. She was smart and serious, so different from the popular cheerleaders he'd typically dated, and that's what drew him to her.

He stepped around the side of the building. "Cate Boudreaux. It's been a long time."

She gasped and turned to face him. Her eyes widened. At least she finally looked him in the eye. She opened and closed her mouth like a fish.

If she didn't want to dance or have anything to do with him, she could've given him a more adult response. A simple no thank you would have been better than coming up with that bullshit. He hated liars. It had no place in his life and was a freaking waste of time. Worse, she'd also made him look like a fool in front of his family. He didn't come to this wedding to be laughed at like some joke. Why the hell did she pull some act like that? Her reaction was over the top. Not fuckin' cool.

He took deep breaths to stay calm. She continued to gape at him, still without a reply. Frozen, like a trapped animal. If he wasn't so pissed, he would have felt sorry for her.

He stepped closer to her. "Why have you been lying to me all night?"

CHAPTER FOUR

CATHERINE

She was caught. Angelo stared at her, awaiting her answer. Her skin flushed.

"You finally figured it out." Catherine raised her chin and ignored her trembling fingers. "Took you long enough."

He reached her in three strides, probing her with an intense gaze. "Why?"

"Hmm, let's see." She tapped her chin. "You hit on me with the insult of not even recognizing me."

He grunted. "I wasn't hitting on you."

"Fine," she conceded with a short wave. "You asked me to dance. It definitely seemed to be heading in that direction."

"And you think that gives you the right to screw with me?"

"I wasn't—" she began but knew that what he was saying was entirely true. Nothing she could say would undo that. "You deserved it." God, now she sounded defensive. Which made sense because she'd had to erect a shield since she saw him tonight.

"I deserved it?" His brows tightened and he pointed at his chest. "Because I didn't recognize you at first?"

"At first." She hmphed with disbelief. "More like at all."

He cocked his head. "You look different."

"Oh, come on, I'm not wearing glasses." She planted her hands on her hips. "Big deal."

"And the hair. I've never seen you wear it like that." He motioned at her tendrils framing her face. "Pinned up with all those curly things, whatever they're called."

She shrugged. "So, my hair's a little different."

"The makeup too." He squinted as he examined her. "You didn't wear makeup when I knew you. Or if you did, it wasn't noticeable."

"You're coming up with excuses now." She raised her index finger and then pointed at him. "I recognized you the second I saw you. Even with the beard covering half your face."

"You win a medal. Happy?" He shook his head. "What do you want from me? It's been ten years."

"Ugh." She spun on the heel of her strappy sandal, which was far from graceful and lacked any dramatic effect on the grass and rushed away.

"How can you be mad?" He reached her within two seconds. "I'm the one who should be pissed at you."

Catherine stopped and faced Angelo. "And why is that?"

"You lied to me. One, about your name. Two, about where you roomed with Diana." He tapped his index finger on his palm, emphasizing the count.

She sought to find a steady hold in her jumbled feelings. "What would you do if you were in my shoes?"

His face turned stony. "I'd probably be mad. But instead of some weird prank, I'd tell you straight out who I was. Not play games."

"I wasn't playing games!" she protested, taking a step toward him. Bad idea. They stood close. Too close. Almost as if they were back in the dance. Her breath came out quicker, pounding in her ears over the music inside.

"Then what *were* you doing?"

Good question. She didn't have a good answer to go with it. The only thing she could think of was self-preservation, which sounded like an over the top reaction. She wasn't so hurt that she wasn't recognized, it was that she wasn't recognized *by him*. No way in hell was she going to admit that to him.

"It was a natural reaction," she said with a casual wave. She had to tone down her heated response so he couldn't see how much he'd hurt her. "I don't know why I said it." She shrugged in an attempt at nonchalance that would hardly offset her strong reaction to him all night. "What can I say? It happened in the moment."

Angelo snorted. "Yeah, my ass it did."

She squirmed at being called out. He wasn't buying her excuse. How much he saw through her she wasn't sure—and she'd be damned before she'd let him pry any deeper. "Now it's my turn to ask the questions, starting with the one I already asked, but you never answered."

"And what was that?"

"How did you finally figure out it was me?"

He studied her for a moment. The ice in his glare melted, softening his intense gaze. Centuries pounded by as she held her breath and waited.

"Your laugh."

Her heart thudded with a loud thump and she closed her eyes. He'd always said how he loved her laugh, and that only he knew the magic tricks to make her smile.

Those two words he'd uttered didn't just clink the shield she'd erected to defend herself, they melted it into liquid metal. She opened her eyes, braving herself to look at him once more.

"I always loved to be the one to break through your seriousness to get you to smile." He cocked his head and gave her a boyish grin. "And when I made you laugh—no greater victory."

Why was he doing this to her? Making her feel so—so—so *much*.

If she didn't do something to protect herself quickly, she was setting herself up for more pain. She'd learned the hard way long ago how charming he could be.

She had to get away from him before all those feelings she'd buried years before came bubbling forth like a test tube with a combustible mix.

"I'm not some prize to celebrate your victory." She raised her chin and turned to head inside. "I need to go."

"What is going on with you, Cate?" He grabbed her wrist with roughness at first, but then he softened it as he rubbed the fleshy part of her thumb in a circular motion.

Heat coursed through her once more. She was slipping. Melting under his touch.

"Don't go like this." Even his voice came out gentler, a low rich tone as smooth as the chocolate fountain in the reception area. He caressed her palm and stepped closer. "Don't go at all."

Damn, she was melting. The frigid exterior that protected her heart splintered with cracks created by his voice alone. What he was doing to her with those words... How could she not be affected?

She scanned their surroundings, seeking purchase before she lost footing, as sure as if the beach was covered with quicksand. They were alone in the dark out here. The sound of the waves came in from one side while a slow song carried in from the band on the other. The crescent moon's reflection danced in the waves. The romantic ambiance of a seaside wedding was too difficult to ignore. And they were steps from the hotel. Rooms and rooms with empty beds. They could be alone in one in a couple of minutes.

"Why?" She heard the tremble in her tone and hoped he didn't catch it.

When she faced him again, his gaze traveled from her eyes to her mouth. She took in a sharp breath, and her lips parted. Was he going to kiss her right there? Would she let him? Did she want him to?

Her heart pounded out each excruciating second.

"Look, I know I screwed up, and I'd be pissed too," he said. "Can we start over?"

His words broke her trance and she blinked.

She sought steady ground amid the heated tension. "All right."

"I didn't mean to hurt you."

Was there any way this conversation could go without amplifying her discomfort? She searched for an escape. "I need to head back inside."

"Why?"

"Bridesmaid duties." The truth was, they'd done all their tasks earlier. Decorated the honeymoon suite with rose petals and all that. Did all their duties during the ceremony and reception. They were probably all in the bag already. A part of her wished she was too. That she'd taken advantage of the open bar and drank enough not to remember this evening. At all.

"Fine," he let go of her hand. "You're staying here at the hotel?"

Was he asking to come up to her room? Catherine rubbed the seam on the side of her dress. She had a room with another bridesmaid, who was probably still inside dancing. She could text her roommate to not return yet, take him upstairs, and live out one of the many fantasies she'd never had a chance to act on. That one night where she almost lost her virginity to him came tumbling back, a moment she'd replayed in her mind hundreds of times. What if she hadn't stopped him?

Flushed from her heated thoughts, she simply nodded her head. She wasn't one for one-night-stands, but maybe one night with him would be what she needed.

Could she pull it off?

"Perfect," he said. "Let's start over again tomorrow. No games."

Tomorrow? Wait, what? What about tonight?

"Have breakfast with me." Angelo trailed his fingers from her hand up her arm.

Despite his touch, her fantasy erupted into hundreds of floating bubbles, like the ones the guests had blown when the bride and groom returned down the aisle. Angelo wasn't proposing spending the night together. Bummer. She sank in a pool of disappointment and relief.

Breakfast. Ah, right. That was probably a better idea than getting naked and sweaty in the sheets with him. More practical than throwing herself into a role of seduction she wasn't quite sure she could play.

But she had to help Diana and Ryan before they headed on their honeymoon and help any wedding guests with travel plans.

"I'm busy until checkout."

"That works."

She couldn't think of an excuse. Scratch that, she didn't want to. After all that had happened tonight with her emotions turning in her mind like clothes tumbling in a dryer, one thought dominated above the rest—excitement.

"Okay."

He smiled in triumph, white teeth dazzling under the moonlight. "I'll look for you at breakfast. 0800."

CATHERINE SPENT THE REST OF THE RECEPTION IN A STUPOR OF going through the motions. She danced, she toasted, she pretended not to steal glances at Angelo. Around midnight, she called it quits and returned to her room. When she set her phone alarm, she remembered that Trent had found another way to contact her.

Last week, he'd sent her a letter at work. He'd rambled on for several pages warning about her project for the government. *"They planted something in my brain that is messing up my memories."* It was difficult to follow the logic. Phrases seemed to be thrown together like they'd come from a refrigerator magnet set with the theme of conspiracy theories.

A few days later he'd sent an email asking if she'd read his letter. She'd reported these incidents to her supervisor, and he noted he'd received them in the past, but nothing ever came from it. He directed her to report it to security. Frank, the security office, confirmed that this guy sent letters to those in the brain department every six months or so. With so much information accessible online, he had probably found her listed as a new project lead and added her to his distribution list.

"I'll forward it on," Frank had said.

Would anything come from that? It was probably as effective as reporting a phishing email. Did anyone act on the info?

"It sounds like he's reaching out for help. He should talk to a professional."

"I'll add that to the report," Frank had added. "Don't respond. It will encourage him to continue the conversation."

When she returned to work on Monday, she'd tell Frank about the latest contact. She had to put it out of her mind if she wanted to get any sleep. Tomorrow, she had a date with Angelo, and she needed a good night's rest. She pictured how he'd looked tonight. So enticing in a suit—fit and confident. And when he'd held her in his arms...

A different kind of anxiety swirled inside, one with excited wings that took flight. Was that good for her or bad?

. . .

ANGELO

SUNDAY MORNING, CATHERINE WOKE BEFORE HER ALARM IN AN unfamiliar bed with fluffy bedding. Sunlight drifted from a gap in the curtains, casting light on a desk near the window. Ah yes, the hotel.

She rubbed her forehead and groaned. A morning of smiling and small talk ahead. Superficial conversations exhausted her. She showered and dressed in a light yellow sundress, preparing for the final leg of her bridesmaid's duties. As she descended to the breakfast area, the scents of eggs and bacon greeted her. And coffee. That would help.

After getting a cup to fortify her, she plastered on a smile, and caught up with the other bridesmaids.

When Diana entered with a brilliant smile and a white summer dress, she pulled Catherine aside. "Did you hook up last night?"

A twinge of regret funneled in Catherine's core. "No. It didn't pan out."

"Aww. Too bad. I was hoping you'd go for it."

"Forget me," Catherine brushed it off with a wave. "This is your wedding. How was your night?"

"Fantastic." Diana's gaze drifted off and a satisfied smile spread. "I'll spare you the details, but I'm one happy newlywed." She waggled her brows. "I'm looking forward to two weeks in Hawaii trying all sorts of new things." Her mischievous smile and arched brow signaled trouble ahead.

"Oh my God, you're going to come back with some sex scandal, aren't you?"

Diana laughed. "Hope so." Then she turned and addressed some family members who entered the breakfast area with the sweetest of smiles.

Several minutes later, Angelo walked in with his family. He wore black slacks and a light gray button-down shirt. They walked over to an available table. When he spotted her, he smiled and headed her way. Catherine's insides lit and nerves flared up like mini fireworks.

"Good morning, Cate." He greeted her with a quick kiss on the cheek.

Her skin heated where his lips had touched, where his beard had tickled her skin. She resisted the urge to place her hand there as if to capture that feeling.

"How did you sleep?" He searched her eyes.

Terrible. How could she get much sleep when she knew she'd see him this morning? Fantasies had spiraled and anticipation had left her near giddy.

She struggled to keep those thoughts from her expression. "Fine. You?"

"Like the dead." He flashed a one-sided smile. "Until my mom made us get up early to return for breakfast. My old bed is a luxury after some of the other places I've stayed in."

The image of him in a bed kick-started last night's fantasies. She shoved them aside and attempted to keep her tone reserved for normal small talk. "You didn't sleep at the hotel?"

He shook his head. "My parents still live in Newport, so it was close enough to go back there."

"Ah, right."

"Come say hi to my folks." He took her hand and he led her through the tables.

She tried to ignore the tingles that spread from fingertips to palm.

He stopped before a seated group and said, "Hey, everyone. Remember Cate? I mentioned how we ran into each other last night."

She recognized them all, although they'd only met a few times. His younger brothers had been in their teens when she'd last seen them, but now they appeared more mature. The youngest had a beard.

"Hey, Cate," the bearded one said. "Nice trick you played on my big brother last night."

Oh no. He knew. What had she been thinking? She shrugged. "It wasn't planned."

"Then you're good on your toes. His ego needs a good take down every so often." He raised an index finger and grinned. "Next time let me in on it. I'd be glad to help out."

She smiled. "I'd be happy to." She'd forgotten their names. Maybe the only thing she'd forgotten when it came to memories of Angelo.

"Oh, would you now, Matty?" Angelo gave him a playful punch on the arm.

"Enough," his mother reprimanded them with her mom look. "This isn't the time to wrestle like Neanderthals." She turned to Catherine and smiled. "Cate. It's been a long time. How have you been?"

"Fine, thanks. And all of you?"

His mother nudged his father's arm, "Don't you remember her? The smart one who was going to MIT."

The smart one. That's what everyone had always said about her as she'd grown up. Cate was the smart one while her taller, willowy older sister with the blonde hair and green eyes was the pretty one. Why not just say Cate was plain. Boring. Invisible.

"Oh yeah," his father said although it was clear he didn't remember. "Good to see you."

Forgettable. She repressed a sigh.

"Can you believe all the boys are in the military?" his mother gushed. "They followed their father into the service. Now he's finally retired, but I have three new reasons to worry. Especially since these two are SEALs and Vince is a Marine."

Damn. Angelo had managed to meet that impressive goal. "Oh, I didn't know that." She faced him. "You did it? Became a SEAL?"

His mother said. "I don't understand you boys. Sometimes your egos are so huge, it's a wonder that they don't blow out the walls of the house. Other times, you're humble."

Angelo turned one hand palm up. "We didn't have a chance to talk about that yet."

His mother turned back to Catherine. "What have you been up to since graduation?"

"I've spent much of that time in school. Now I'm an assistant professor and neuroscientist in Providence."

After a few more minutes of small talk, including exchanging information on who they knew in the wedding and how, Cate excused herself. "It was nice to see you all again."

Angelo followed her back through the tables of guests. Once they moved away from the din of conversation, he said, "When you're done, how about we head over to the Cliff Walk? It's going to be a beautiful July day."

"Sure." She forced a casual nod, while frissons of delight danced through her. They'd be alone on a romantic walk. The trail was a noted feature of Newport that hugged the shore with brilliant vistas of the ocean on one side, and then nature with the opulent Newport mansions on the other.

"Did you bring a car?" Angelo asked. "I came with my family."

"Yes. I'll meet you out front at check out."

She glanced at her outfit and assessed the appropriateness for the activity. A sundress with sandals, but that might not cut it. "I can change into sneakers." She tossed her hair over her shoulder and grinned. "Since you are a badass SEAL, I'm guessing you'd choose a more challenging route over a leisurely walk. Maybe some treacherous climb up rocks or something."

He laughed and shook his head. "I don't care where we go. I just want to spend time with you."

A quick flush of heat rose. "I'll change into something better suited for walking."

"Good plan. I will too."

That trembling sensation inside returned—a wild mix of anxiety and excitement leaving her on unsteady footing. Maybe this was a bad idea.

Too damn bad.

No way would she back out now. She'd already had ten years of speculation packed up like storage in her mind. No more wondering. She was going to be bold today, let him know she wanted him.

Would reality live up to the fantasy?

CHAPTER FIVE

ANGELO

Fifteen minutes before it was time to check out, Angelo paced the grounds in front of the venue, absently circling a massive fragrant flower bed with blue hydrangeas and pink and white flowers. It was ridiculous how much he was looking forward to seeing her again. He still hadn't gotten over her ruse last night, but she had a semi-legit reason. He couldn't fault her there. She had pride and she stood up for herself. He would have done the same thing. Although not taking the same tactic.

When she came outside, wearing tan shorts and a blue tank top that clung to her perfectly rounded breasts, he sucked in a breath. Seeing her in the bridesmaid's dress last night was something else, and she looked so pretty in a pale-yellow sundress at breakfast. But now in sneakers and casual summer clothes, she was even hotter.

"Ready?" she asked.

He gave her another long appraisal, not masking his interest. "Am I ever."

A blush rose in her cheeks. She swatted him on the arm. "If you keep looking at me like that, I may run off."

Taking her by the arm, he linked his with hers. "Then I better hold onto you."

He was flirting, but since she smiled back, he chalked it up as a good sign. Still, he had to rein it in. He couldn't come on too strong and pounce on her, no matter how strong the urge. She wasn't a bridesmaid he sought out for a quick hookup. She was Cate. Cate Boudreaux.

"Come on, Romeo." She led him to a dark green Prius.

He threw his backpack in the back seat. It had snacks and water for the day ahead—and a change of underwear and a toothbrush, just in case. Probably wishful thinking. He squeezed into the passenger seat.

Cate turned on the car and the sounds of the local NPR station filled the car. She turned it down and drove from the estate.

He glanced at her. "Today, I want us to start fresh. No games, okay?"

Her lips parted and then she sighed. "Okay."

She took the scenic route, hugging the coastline. He gazed out to the sea. He'd taken this view for granted growing up here. After countless assignments in the desert surrounded by sand, the sea calmed him more than ever.

"I didn't know you're a neuroscientist."

"I am." She kept her eyes on the road ahead.

A one-word answer followed by two. How could he convince her to open up?

"Tell me about it, Cate. I want to know what you've been up to."

"Oh, you know. School, work. Lots of research on the brain, which makes most people's eyes glaze over." She waved and then planted her hand back on the steering wheel. "How long are you on leave for?"

Interesting. She evaded answering his questions and quickly turned the line of questioning on to him. Why? He'd have to play her game and move forward at her pace. They didn't need a repeat of last night with heated emotions.

"A week from this Wednesday." Only ten more days. Leave always rushed by far too quickly.

She glanced at him before turning back to the road. Was that a flicker of disappointment in her eyes? That gave him a glimmer of hope.

For what? He wasn't entirely sure.

"Where to after that?" she asked.

"I'm stationed in Little Creek, Virginia. But, we're shipped out more than we're there."

He stared out the window. Sailboats and yachts dotted the harbor. The familiar coast brought back memories. Although he'd visited many port towns during his ten years in the Navy, Newport was unlike any other. The time stamp of the gilded age with the Newport mansions and historic homes of naval officers stood ever present among more modern developments in the city.

Nostalgia swept through him like a grandmother flipping pages of a yellowed photo album. When his father had been home, he'd taken them sailing on summer weekends. Sometimes they'd even go fishing. They'd head to the wharves, which were always lively with pubs, restaurants, and shops.

"Angelo?"

"Yes?"

"Oh good, you're still with me."

What an odd statement. He faced her. "What do you mean?"

"I just asked you if you wanted anything from the store." She nodded her chin toward a convenience store. "You didn't answer."

"Oh. Sorry. I was somewhere else for a minute."

"Where?"

How could he explain it? "It's been a long time since I've been back in Newport. Seeing parts of it reminds me of—home."

She glanced at him and returned her focus on the road. "You've been gone so long. Is it still where you consider home?"

It had been a good ten years since he lived here. Funny how long ago that seemed although he was only 28. He'd spent his middle and high school years here, formative years, so no matter how many times they'd moved in the early part of his father's naval career, Angelo still felt the connection to Newport.

"I haven't lived in anyplace for more than a couple of years since leaving here. So yes, I guess this is—and might always be —home."

"It must be difficult to move so often. Is it?"

"Sometimes," he admitted. "It's a life I signed up for, so I can't complain. I knew what I was getting myself into."

"What do you remember about growing up here?"

"Some of the bigger weeks, like the jazz festival and regatta. We loved to watch the races. And nothing beats Christmas in Newport. The town is decked out in lights, and the smell of cookies seems everywhere. But mostly just being with my family."

"Oh." She moaned and covered her heart. "Now I feel like I'm keeping you from them."

"Are you kidding me?" He chuckled. "I spent the last couple of days with them. No need to smother each other."

She sighed. "You assuaged my guilt." She smiled. "Since I'm a driver at your disposal today, I'm happy to take you around. What would you like to see?"

You.

That sudden thought made him shift in the seat. He wouldn't say it. No point in coming on too strong.

"Let's start at Forty Steps and take it from there."

"Sounds great."

She parked near the granite steps, a local attraction with access to the Cliff Walk. They descended to the walking path and the vast expanse of the ocean stretched before them.

He took a deep inhale. "I took this scent for granted when I was younger. Multiple deployments changed that, and I don't let that happen anymore."

She tilted her head. "I can imagine." Straightening it again, she added, "Actually, I can't. I'd never be cut out for military life."

His jaw twitched. That meant she wouldn't be up for a relationship with someone in the military either. He shook his head to snap himself out of that. Why even think like that?

They walked in silence along the shoreline for a few moments, passing couples from the opposite direction. Seagulls called as they flew overhead. He wanted to take her hand, but that might be pushing it.

"What's it like?" she said, breaking the silence. "I'm guessing it's pretty brutal to be a SEAL."

He shrugged. "It's not easy. But like anything else, you get used to it. Once you know what's expected of you—and what you can expect from that lifestyle—you learn to adjust."

"For instance?"

"I know that I could be called out at any moment, so I need to be ready to leave. When my family gets the chance to spend time together, it makes it more special."

She sighed. "You're making me feel guilty again."

"Hey," he said with a laugh. "I'm with them all week. We all need some fresh air—and a break from each other."

They passed one of the mansions along the route. His mother loved taking them to visit the mansions when they were younger, especially during the holidays when they were decked out in lights and smelled like Christmas.

Cate pointed to it. "I guess that's why some families think they need a house that size."

He laughed. "Still might not be big enough for mine with all our egos."

Her brows tightened. "You were always confident, but you never came off as cocky."

"I can't deny that I have my share of pride. But I know when to back off. The team comes first."

That had been his mindset for years. His entire life revolved around the SEALs. He lived it, worked it, and breathed it. Which was why he'd told himself he didn't have room in his life for a relationship. It was too difficult to balance a military career with family obligations, he knew that all too well.

"Do you each have different roles?"

"Yes, I'm a corpsman, so in addition to my SEAL duties, I take care of the team's medical needs."

She turned and raised her brows. "Really?"

"No lie. It took years of training, including a special ops combat medic course."

"That must be—intense." Her voice softened, the way it often did when people envisioned what he might have gone through. "You've probably seen more than I could ever imagine."

Had he ever. A flash of Donovan returned. Before he let the memory overwhelm him, he snapped his attention to the surrounding scenery with the sunlight glimmering on the water. "True. But it's a beautiful day and I'd prefer not talk about some ugly things."

"Understood," she said in a gentle tone. "Is there anything in particular you'd like to talk about?"

He gave her a one-sided grin, eager to change to a lighter topic before he ruined their afternoon with a somber mood. "How I've lucked out spending the day with a gorgeous woman."

An adorable shade of pink spread across her cheeks, and she glanced away as if flustered by the compliment.

"Is anyone going to be pissed off that you're here with me?" he asked.

"Meaning a boyfriend or husband?"

"Yes."

"Nooo." She frowned. "I wouldn't be here with you if there was."

"Just making sure." Being married hadn't stopped people he'd known from finding someone on the side.

"I'm a single woman who lives with two kittens." She arched her brows. "What a cliché."

He laughed, mostly with relief that she was single. "It's all a matter of how you look at it. How about you're a badass neuroscientist who wrangles two mischievous felines?"

"The wrangling is right. Mischievous is also accurate. I never knew how wild two kittens could be. I've had cats before, but these two feed off each other's energy."

"How old are they?"

"Almost a year. Maybe they'll calm down soon. I have my neighbor checking in on them while I'm here. So far, no calls that they've destroyed the place. So, there's that."

"You're not home yet. They could have done some major damage while you were gone."

She swatted his bicep. "Thanks for the vote of confidence."

He glanced at her hand, wishing she'd kept it on his arm. "I've lived with various pets growing up. When they're quiet, that means trouble."

She clucked her tongue. "How true."

He brushed his fingers over her bare shoulder, unable to keep from touching her. "I can't believe I ran into you after all the years—and finding someone hasn't snatched you up. You're smart. Sophisticated. Sexy. Sassy…"

Her lips curled into a semi-smile. "I like the alliteration."

"And sarcastic."

She laughed. "Snappy." With a quick glance at him, she said, "What about you? No wife or girlfriend?"

"Nope."

"Why not?"

"Military life is tough, especially for the person who stays home. I already have my mom worried about me. I can't put another woman through that."

She glanced at him with a speculative expression. "Still, some couples make it work, right?"

"Yeah, some of my teammates are married and have kids. I don't know how they do it. Not only would I feel guilty about all the worrying I'd cause, but…" He paused, not sure he should finish what he'd started to say.

"But what?"

He stared out to the ocean and exhaled. "I've seen a lot of cheating. People getting lonely, maybe. Or jealous. Wondering about that might drive me crazy."

A few seconds passed before she responded. "I guess you'd need to find the right partner. Someone you could trust completely with your heart." Her expression turned wistful.

Exactly. "An elusive discovery." He grunted and added, "Not that I've been looking."

He glanced at her and their gazes locked. He heated from the inside out while his brains scrambled, sizzling like an egg being dropped on the pavement at midday in Kabul.

No. Time to get a grip. He broke the gaze. "Enough about me. Now it's your turn to spill."

She didn't answer right away. Would she?

"You knew I was planning on going to MIT, and I did. Then I earned my doctorate at Brown, focusing on brain science."

Not only had she pursued her goal to study at MIT, she'd gone beyond it and earned her doctorate. Admirable. That was one of the things that drew him to Cate back in high school—her intelligence. She was different from the other girls. They could talk on the phone and never run out of conversation.

"What made you go into that field?" he asked.

She let out a soft exhale. "I know it's been a long time, but do you remember what happened with my cousins?"

His mind raced back there, and once he remembered, it all made sense. "One had epilepsy, another a tumor, which turned out to be cancer."

"Exactly." Her demeanor darkened and worry etched in her expression.

Now for the difficult follow-up question. He swallowed. "Are they all right?"

"They are." A relieved smile passed over her face, and like an ocean wave, it was gone. "They're both in high school now. One should have graduated by now, but he missed a lot of school during the treatments."

"I can see why you'd want to learn more about the brain," he said.

"Right." She turned to face him and gestured with her hands. "They're the reason I started to learn about it when I was younger—and the inspiration for me to want to help people with brain issues. The more we understand how it functions, the better we can treat conditions like what my cousins had to endure. Maybe even prevent them from ever happening. I'm mapping out areas with technology and conducting experiments to see how we can encourage other parts of the brain to adapt and take on functions of damaged areas, like memory in Alzheimer's patients."

As she spoke, her eyes brightened and her tone turned excited, showing passion for her work. What a difference from how she'd seemed closed off about it minutes before.

"That's impressive, Cate," he replied. "So many warfighters suffer traumatic brain injury. We're always trying to improve medical treatment on the battlefield. You want to save everyone you can."

Her gaze fixed on his, as if seeing right into him. "But sometimes you can't."

His throat tightened. He cleared it. Before they probed that topic deeper, he had to steer away. If she could do that, so could he. "You work in Providence?"

"Right, at a university. Although I teach, I'm still learning. There's so much we still don't know about the brain. And if we did, it could lead to tremendous advances, not just in medical treatment for kids like my cousins, but other areas of health care." With a nod in his direction, she added, "Even for military and veterans."

He gulped. "Like PTSD?"

"Yes, exactly. Once you understand what the brain needs and how it functions, you can help it heal. Memory is one aspect that fascinates me. Intuition is another." She studied him with a keen gaze. "Do you ever get a sense that something is wrong, without knowing why?"

Angelo's muscles tensed. Hell, he'd experienced it on the mission with Donovan. The hair on the back of his neck had raised as they traversed the dense forest in South America.

Something had been wrong. What, he couldn't place. It had gone beyond situational awareness.

Moments later, their team had been ambushed. Enemies attacked from out of nowhere, like camouflaged ghosts haunting the jungle. Everything turned FUBAR. Donovan had been hit. The gash on his abdomen hadn't been pretty. The prognosis didn't look good.

Angelo attempted to treat the wound, taking slow breaths while bullets whipped past his ears. The scent of gunfire engulfed the surrounding forest. Cold sweat drenched his overheated body and his fingers trembled.

"I've got you, Donovan. You're going to be okay."

A damn lie. Donovan bled out on the jungle floor. Angelo's face was the last he had seen.

"Are you all right, Angelo?"

He snapped back to the present at the sound of her voice and her hand on his shoulder. His heart slammed against his ribs as if he were still there in the forest. It had all been so vivid.

Catherine watched him with a concerned expression, and then moved to pull her hand away. He placed his hand on top of hers, keeping it there. His skin felt too hot. Too tight. Too clammy.

He took measured breaths and scanned his surroundings. They were near the ocean in Newport. Not in some jungle fighting off an ambush.

Shaking the disturbing memory off like it was an unwanted blanket in a blazing hot desert, he replied. "Yes, I'm fine." He released a shaky exhale. "I was thinking about what you said."

"I'm sorry if I said something that upset you."

Shit, he had to get himself together. He couldn't unravel in front of Cate. He released her hand and squeezed his hands into fists. Fuck. The doubts slipped in, the ones that slithered like eels making him question how much longer he could do this. This leave was a test of sorts. If he could recuperate during leave, he'd be able to return to his team and function the way they needed him. The entire team looked up to the corpsman. After all, he'd be the one to try to save their asses when it came down to it. He couldn't lose his edge. If so, he'd no longer be an asset to the team.

Compartmentalize. Look around you and come back to the present.

He fixed his gaze on Cate and forced himself to lighten the sudden somber vibe. "Forget about it. I was thinking how good you got me yesterday," he lied. "If my team finds out, I'd never hear the end of it."

Her cheeks turned pink. "I won't tell."

"Where did you come up with that story?"

Cate flinched. Her eyes darkened.

"What's wrong?"

"Nothing." She brushed at her tank top like she was removing something, which he guessed was nonexistent.

"Did I say something?"

"No." Every part of her appeared to tense, from the tightness in her lips to her straight spine.

What had he said that triggered her response? "Something seems off. If you don't want to tell me, Cate, I get it. I haven't been a part of your life, and I have no business asking you personal questions." Plus, he'd just evaded revealing what bothered him to her and then straight up lied. He grimaced at the hypocrisy.

Although it was none of his business, it bothered him. He had to know things. And when he didn't, he'd continued to poke at it until he found out. But he wouldn't push her and kill their day together.

"It's not that." The strange tone of her voice made him stop to face her. She stopped walking.

"What is it?" he asked. "Are you afraid of something?"

She shook her head and then bit her lip. Her troubled expression indicated she might be wrestling with something. She took a deep breath and exhaled with a catch in her sigh.

"Yes, I'm afraid." She stepped closer so they were less than a foot apart. She stared up at him with vulnerability in her eyes.

"Of what?"

Her breath quickened, breasts rising and falling. She continued to stare into his eyes and the mood changed. Heat engulfed him, entirely separate from the summer sun. She lifted her hand and ran it over his beard with a gentle caress.

"Regrets." Her eyelids lowered and her voice turned breathy.

Being so close to her, gazing into her eyes, having her look at him like that—it left him taut with anticipation.

"Regrets?" he repeated.

Her gaze lowered to his mouth and she leaned toward him. Instinct drove him to lower his head in what seemed like slow motion. Her warm breath fanned his face. With their lips only inches apart, she exhaled with a soft sigh. That tiniest of sounds affected him more than he thought possible.

"I'm afraid of walking away and then I'll drown in wonder and regret." She rose to her tiptoes and moved a hairbreadth from his lips. "Not this time."

CHAPTER SIX

CATHERINE

The instant Catherine's lips touched Angelo's, sparks ignited. Every nerve ending seemed to flare with life.

Had she really been the one to make the first move? They were on a public walkway along the cliffs where anyone could walk by! This was so unlike her, and the first time she'd been so bold. What was it about Angelo? Since she had run into him yesterday, her thoughts were so confused, as if her brain was forging new neural pathways. Their conversation had turned intense. When he'd asked about how she'd come up with her act, she had to end that conversation. Trent's intrusions had invaded enough of her head space. She wasn't going to let it interfere with what might be her only chance to reconnect with Angelo.

It was time to shut her overanalytical mind off and be in the moment. Finally experience what she'd fantasized about for years.

When he pressed his tongue to the seam of her mouth, she opened her lips wider, and their tongues clashed. He tasted clean with the faint hint of minty toothpaste.

He wrapped his arms around her, pulling her body against his. A new wave of heat pulsed through her, intensifying within her core. She ran her fingers through his hair, moaning softly into his mouth. With the other hand, she trailed her fingers over the back of his neck.

She was so damn glad she listened to her body this time instead of letting her head get in the way.

After all these years, she was kissing Angelo again. It was even better than she'd remembered, and more romantic than she'd fantasized with the seaside setting. They devoured each other in this kiss as if it had been building up for ten years.

Well, it had—for her.

She lost herself in the kiss, but then strove to imprint every detail to memory. The romantic glow from the sun warming their skin and twinkling on the water. His beard fanning her face, so different from the last time they'd kissed when he had been clean-shaven. The sound of the waves crashing against the rocks and the salty scent permeated the air. The touch of his hands as he stroked her lower back left a trail of heat burning through her. Even the soft brush of his hair under her fingertips affected her in a strange way deep within.

And there was no mistaking his excitement when he pressed against her. It sent a wave of wet heat in between her legs.

The sound of giggles nearby barely registered.

Angelo pulled away from her. "Come on, we should get moving."

She gasped for air. It took a couple of seconds for his words to sink in. Go where? And why? She was content to stay where they were, kissing Angelo for eternity.

A glimpse at the passersby on the trail who cast quick glances at them sobered her. Ah, right. They were in public. There were middle-school girls nearby, giggling as they shot glances over.

Hot damn. Her cheeks heated. What a blatant public display of affection, something she would never, ever do.

A slow smile spread across her face. It had been worth it.

An hour later, they were seated outside at a seaside restaurant on the wharf with a view of the ocean. Seagulls flew nearby, likely searching to scavenge for a scrap of fallen seafood. A gentle breeze caressed Catherine's skin. She breathed in the ocean scent, hoping it would calm her racing pulse.

She had to center herself. Her reaction to him was too volatile. She stirred her cup of clam chowder, whisking the oyster crackers around until they were buried.

She'd agreed to spend the day with Angelo. But, what about the night?

He took a bite of the clam chowder and her gaze drifted to his mouth. His lips were right there. If they both leaned across the table…

"What are you thinking about?" He eyed her with speculation.

She snapped out of her ruminations and stirred with more vigor. "Nothing. Nothing at all."

The way he continued to appraise her indicated he knew she was full of it. She struggled to not let her emotions control her reaction. What was happening in her body was just a biological drive for reproduction. The attraction consuming her mind was simply a chemical reaction.

Don't overthink this.

Why couldn't she let go and enjoy herself? If she could brush off her inhibitions and avoid over-analyzing the implications, she could invite him back to her place for the night and do the things she regretted not doing with him ten years ago. Hadn't she waited long enough?

"You look like you're worried about something."

"I'm just—" She released the spoon. "Thinking."

"About?" he prodded.

Clearly, he wasn't going to let it go.

She leaned back in her chair and smoothed invisible wrinkles from her tank top. "Do you ever think about the night before you left?"

He grunted. "Of course. That was my last night as a civilian. I was scared shitless about what I was about to get myself into."

"I mean—what happened—or almost happened, with us."

He put his spoon down. "Oh. That."

The back of her neck tensed. Why had she brought that up? It was a decade ago. Stupid. So stupid.

"Of course." His voice lowered to a smooth, dark timbre.

She glanced up, not knowing what to expect. His deep brown eyes were warm as they probed hers, locking her in. She seemed to sink into his gaze, the intensity of it was too much.

"I wish things had gone differently that night," she admitted.

Her face warmed. Had she just blurted that out? Damn him and his penetrating stare, drawing the truth out from where she'd buried it many years ago.

"Me too," he said. "But you weren't ready."

True. But it would have been better to lose her virginity to him, someone she cared about, rather than during an awkward encounter with a college friend. Then again, with Angelo it might have left her heart in more splintered pieces when he went away. It had been devastating enough.

With a deep inhale, she resolved not to sink back into the vulnerabilities of a young girl smitten by first love. She was a successful, independent woman. She could do things differently now. She could state what she wanted.

Catherine rehearsed her words before she said them. "I don't want things to end the same way tonight."

His eyes flickered with question as he measured her. "What are you saying, Cate?"

You can do this. It's simply stating what you want. Don't complicate things. It's not brain surgery.

She raised her chin. "I want you to come home with me tonight."

Angelo's eyes widened. The server arrived with their meals—a surf and turf dinner for him and a baked scrod for her. The appetizing scent of the seafood was lost amid the rapid heat spreading through her body. Her statement loomed between them, heavy with tension, as she waited for his reply.

Once the server left, Angelo asked, "You sure about this?"

"Absolutely. Why wouldn't I be?"

He leaned forward. "Because I'm leaving next week."

She squirmed in her chair. "I know."

He searched her eyes. "Which means—I'm gone."

Why was he repeating that? Because they lived in two different worlds, far from each other? Right. It would be insane to expect anything more.

"I'm aware of that." She scrunched up her face. Maybe she was bombing with her attempt at seduction. "Jeez, I didn't expect this reaction. Thought guys jumped for sex when it's on the table."

He burst into laughter. "I didn't know you were offering it up here." He motioned around him and then to their table. "On the table."

"You know what I mean."

His lips tightened into a straight line. "I don't want to lead you on."

She fidgeted with her napkin. "You won't. I know you're leaving and that this is only for one night."

"Good. Because I don't want to hurt you." He glanced into her eyes. "Ever."

Her pulse quickened. "You won't, Angelo. I'm a big girl now. No, a grown woman. I wouldn't have asked you if I didn't want to. Actually, now I'm starting to regret it, as I'm afraid you'll turn me down."

He raised his brows. "Never. No regrets." He pointed to her plate. "Let's eat so we can get out of here." With a smoldering gaze, he added, "We'll take dessert to go."

. . .

CATHERINE'S HEART THRUMMED IN HER EARS AS SHE DROVE BACK to her place. The late afternoon sun cast a gentle glow on the road. Even so, driving was a challenge. How could she focus on the road with Angelo beside her?

And what they had planned.

A small analytical voice in the back of her mind asked if she was setting herself up to get hurt. She all but snapped at it to shut the hell up. But it was still there. A part of her that would always think and question and analyze.

When he placed his hand on her knee, she almost veered out of her lane. She pinned her gaze ahead.

"You okay, Cate?" Angelo asked.

"Fine," she replied automatically, although her voice sounded not quite like her own.

"You seem—nervous." He sounded concerned.

"Nervous?" she repeated with a shaky laugh. Great. That sounded believable.

"Are you changing your mind?"

"No!" Jeez, why not come straight out and tell him she was itching out of her skin just thinking of spending the night with him. Could she sound any more eager? "I mean, no."

"Good." He ran his fingers in slow circles up to her thigh. She couldn't think of anything else, but how good it felt, how much she wanted him to continue. How much higher would he go? After several seconds of hanging on the edge and almost losing her damn mind, she blurted out, "As much as I like that, it's far too distracting while I'm driving."

He chuckled and pulled his hand away. Her thigh cooled with the sudden absence. Yes, she already regretted it. Stupid brain. She multi-tasked all the damn time. Yet she couldn't focus on driving because a man's hand was on her leg?

No, not any man's hand. Angelo's.

"No worries," he said. "We have all night."

That was why she could barely think straight. She blew out a breath to help her relax.

Focus. Don't fantasize.

That was easy to tell herself, much less easy to follow. Not with all the palpable sexual tension that seemed to swell through the interior of the car. Her car had never been the scene of such excitement before, but here she was practically panting like a teenager in heat, ready to dive into the back seat.

Diversion, that's what she needed. "Why don't you find something on the radio?"

He navigated through the channels. "Nothing I hate more than the mindless drivel with commercials."

A man was talking in a super-fast voice, one of those disclaimer spiels at the end of commercials. Although she hated that, anything that would drown out the questions in her head would be a relief. All she wanted to do was turn off her brain for once and focus on what her body was screaming for. Which right now was Angelo DeMarchis.

He stopped on a song. *Stressed Out* by Twenty-One Pilots. Stressed was one way to put it. Anxious was another. Breathless with need might be another.

They arrived at her place, and she parked in the lot. She reached out to open the door.

Angelo put his hand on hers. "Hold on a sec."

She turned to him. "What is it?"

His eyes were dark with hunger. "What I've been thinking about since I sat in this car. You."

Her breathing hitched. Could he have been as affected as she'd been the entire drive?

He cupped her chin and leaned across the seat. "I've wanted to kiss you." Brushing his lips on hers, he then whispered, "Like this."

His slight touch was like a heated whisper over her skin, calling to her, waking her body. Shivers of excitement followed, rippling through her. His touch set her ablaze, and she responded to him with an urgency never before felt.

The kiss quickly intensified, and they grabbed at each other in the front seat. He pulled his mouth from hers, and then kissed along her jawline and over her neck. Warm tingles spread through her. She wanted him, needed him, now. If they didn't move inside, she would pull him in on top of her begging for him there in her car.

What was wrong with her? This was ridiculous. They weren't teenagers any longer.

She dragged herself from the heady haze that clouded her thoughts. "We should go inside."

He murmured against the hollow of her neck, "I know."

It took all her willpower to pull the keys out of the ignition and open the car door. But better things awaited them inside, of that she was certain.

As they walked to her front door, she said, "I'll let you in. I need to tell my neighbor I'm back. She's been watching the cats." She couldn't have Maria interrupting if she heard movement over at her place—not if the night went the way she hoped. "Make yourself at home."

He nodded, heat burning through his gaze. She let him in her house and then tried not to skip on the pathway to Maria's door.

Anticipation fueled her every step. Angelo was waiting for her inside. Soon to be in her bed.

CHAPTER SEVEN

ANGELO

Angelo tried to ignore his erection as he entered Cate's place. He had pounced on her in the car like they were eighteen again. He attempted to shift his focus by seeing where she lived.

A classical music station played at a low volume. For her cats? It also had a hint of vanilla scent in the air. He walked through the pale-yellow galley kitchen and into a dining area with a round wooden table and desk. Her pens were lined up parallel to the edge of the desk. He smiled as it brought back a memory. She'd be rattled if a ballpoint pen was left open and had to shut it. He'd click them open to tease her and get a reaction. A stupid high school antic to get her attention.

He continued into the living room. Her furnishings were tasteful. An overstuffed beige sofa had maroon pillows arranged perfectly straight and uniform and the polished coffee table had a few books arranged perfectly as well. She was neat. That wasn't a surprise.

Where was the bedroom? He peered up the stairs. The sound of tiny footsteps caught his attention. Two cats—one an orange tabby and the other a tuxedo that was mostly black save for white on its chest and paws—came bounding down the stairs and trotted into the living room. They circled around him at first, as if sizing him up, before the orange one rubbed against his leg. He bent down and rubbed under its chin.

"Hello. So, you're one of Cate's roommates."

The other cat remained wary, watching from the foot of the stairs. He opened his hand and called it over, but it turned away from him and walked away tail in the air. He laughed. Hard to win over. That was okay. He knew a few tricks. On the counter, he spotted a container of tuna flavored cat treats tucked neatly in a container. The way to get on a cat's good side was with food. He offered them each a couple. The orange cat darted over to them, but the tuxedo cat watched him with wariness before strutting over and claiming the edible treasures.

How strange it was to be here in Cate's house. What luck to run into her at the wedding. One problem that tugged at the back of his mind was how it could complicate things. When it came to Cate, nothing about his feelings had ever been carefree. Their connection had been deeper. But now they were older and not as naïve about the world. Would that change anything?

The front door opened, and Cate entered. Oxygen zapped from his lungs. She hung her bag on a hook and removed her sneakers, placing them on a mat near the entrance.

He gulped the air. "Everything okay?"

"Yes, everything's fine."

Both cats ran over to her. The tuxedo one didn't seem to have the same wariness it had around Angelo. Cate knelt and talked to them while she rubbed their cheeks and showered them with attention. She turned to mush around them. A smile spread across his face.

He removed his sneakers and placed them on the mat beside hers. "I gave them a few treats. Hope that's okay."

She glanced at him. "They'll love you forever." Her smile was radiant.

A strange warming sensation heated his chest.

"This is Ruby." She rubbed the orange tabby's chin. "And this one is Aurora." When Cate touched Aurora's cheek, she leaned into Cate's palm. After she rose, she asked, "Can I get you a drink?

He caught her gaze. Heat returned, growing more palpable in this space where they were alone. He swallowed. "All I want right now is you."

Damn, could he be any more obvious?

Her eyes brimmed with excitement. She took a few steps toward him, but then hesitated. He closed the remaining distance.

He moved her dark hair over her shoulders and then cupped her face. "You're beautiful, Cate. More so than ever." Then he bent down and kissed her, gently at first, but then as deep and searing as he had in the car.

So much for taking it slow.

She didn't seem to mind since she wrapped her arms around his neck and pressed her body against his. Finally.

Their kiss grew more insistent, igniting a raw need that threatened to consume him. They broke apart, staring at each other as they panted for oxygen. It didn't take long for his erection to return.

The dark sensuality that sparkled in her eyes almost leveled him. A heated magnetism pulsed in the space between them like nothing he'd ever known before. Primal need took over. He needed to touch her.

He kissed her neck, drinking in her taste and scent. He ran his hand down her back and over her ass. Lowering his fingers, he reached up under her shorts and touched her soft skin. Damn, he wanted more. Those shorts teased him by giving him just a peek. Trailing his other hand up the side of her body, he paused to caress her beautiful breasts, which had tempted him all day in that tank top.

She moaned, ending with a delicious sigh of pleasure that encouraged him to continue. He reached under her top and traveled up her soft torso until he felt the delicate lace of her bra.

He reached around and unclasped it without too much trouble. A sweet victory. Then he cupped her full, round breast and thumbed her hardening nipple.

Her breath came out in a jagged gasp. She leaned towards him. "Let's go upstairs."

He couldn't think of a better idea. "Lead the way."

He followed her up the stairs, eyes dropping to her rear. It took all his control not to pounce. When they entered her room, his gaze flickered to the bed. It had a lavender bedspread and tons of white pillows. She turned to him with expectant eyes and moistened, parted lips.

"I should put on some music." She broke the gaze and fumbled with a music player. Seconds later, a woman sang at a low volume. A version of *Dream On*.

"Postmodern jukebox." She shrugged. "I've been listening to it a lot lately."

"I like it." He did like Aerosmith, but he didn't give a shit about what music was on at the moment. Not with this ache that had been building all day.

He wrapped his arms around her and claimed her mouth once more as he backed her toward the bed. In the next moment, he was on top of her, pulling her top off over her head. With her bra unfastened, it was easy to remove and toss aside.

She crossed her arms as if self-conscious.

"No need to do that." He brushed her hands with a feather-light touch. "You're beautiful. Let me see all of you."

She hesitated. "Okay." Her voice came breathy. She slowly lowered her arms, revealing her full breasts.

He bent back down to kiss her. Her hardened nipples pressed against his chest. She wrapped her arms around his back and then tugged at the bottom of his shirt. After he leaned back to unbutton it, they worked together to free him of this obstacle. The slow, delicious way her gaze raked over his upper body made him puff out his chest more.

"I see you work out often."

"Part of the job requirements."

"A bonus for me." Her appreciative smile rocked him with tremors of anticipation.

Cate bit her lower lip as she gazed at him. That movement shot a strange reaction inside him with waves of nervous energy.

She reached for his shorts, with that same intense expression. Once she unfastened the button, she unzipped. Damn, watching her undress him was so fuckin' hot. He'd probably jerked off to a similar image countless times in high school.

This was nothing like high school. They'd both grown up. Cate's womanly body and willingness to take things further were a hell of a turn on. Hell yes, he was on board with this new Cate.

When she tugged at his shorts, he stepped in to roll them down over his hips. His erection tented the front of his boxers. She dropped her gaze and swallowed.

Angelo lowered himself, careful not to crush her, and covered her mouth with his. Her body pressed against his as he tasted her sweet lips.

Even the way they kissed was more adult. None of that awkward fumbling of teenage years, with the push and pull between them. This time, Cate knew exactly what she wanted.

If that gentle moan told him anything, she wanted him. He ran his hands down the front of her body, touching her soft skin. Sliding down, he kissed and licked from her neck down to her breasts. He caressed them. So full, so damn delicious. He took one in his mouth and swirled his tongue around the hardening bud. She squirmed and let out a moan of pleasure. He turned his focus to the other one.

He wanted to savor her breasts all day, yet explore every inch of her body, which had been out of reach for so long. The way she clutched at him and arched her lower body indicated she was just as desperate as he was.

He reached down and caressed the soft skin above her shorts. He unbuttoned them. "Let's get these off."

She arched up to help him with the process. Once they were removed, she lay there in a tiny pair of pink cotton panties with a fringe of white lace. His cock throbbed with more need.

He touched her over the soft fabric between her legs. Then he slipped his finger beneath the seam of her panties and stroked her. She felt like hot, wet silk. He tugged the panties down over her hips and removed them. A glimpse of her glistening pink flesh made him throb. She was beautiful. Desperate for skin on skin contact, he quickly shed the rest of his clothes.

Climbing on her again, he rubbed himself against her folds.

"Condom?" She searched his eyes with the weighted question. If he didn't have one, things could cool off as quick as a blizzard wind.

"I've got one."

He reached for his discarded shorts and fumbled around to find his wallet. Her chest rose and fell with quickened breaths as she watched him. With her cheeks flushed and lips parted, the desire in her expression amped the anticipation.

He fumbled to get the damn condom on and then returned to her. He took her mouth in a long, deep kiss as he slid into her. Damn, she was tight. Thank God he had the condom, or he would've blown his load right away. She felt so good.

So right.

Fuck. That wasn't a thought he should have. Not when this might only be a one-time thing.

CATHERINE

She was with Angelo, at last. How many times had Catherine fantasized about it? Dreamed about it? And now, it was finally happening. The real thing was far more potent. Every move of their hips brought them closer together. Still, she wanted more of him. She wrapped her arms and legs around him, never wanting this to end.

"You feel so good, Cate." He murmured against her neck, a smooth velvet murmur that sent shivers of delight through her. "Worth the wait."

Worth the wait. Those words echoed in her head. God, he was right. She was already on the precipice of losing control. Although she'd tried to distance herself emotionally from this encounter and label it as a one-night hookup, he was making it difficult. Or, perhaps it was her. After yearning for something and then finally getting it, was it possible to enjoy it from a safe distance?

Probably not.

"I know, Angelo. I've wanted you for so long," she admitted.

Why was she saying this? This was just a fling. A glorious, delicious, mind-blowing encounter. Angelo wasn't available to her, physically or emotionally. He'd told her that, and she knew the terms.

Angelo's thrusts grew more intense, blissfully distracting her from her thoughts. She gripped his buttocks and raised her hips against his to pull him inside her deeper still. He pumped harder, driving into her with wild thrusts that made her cry out. The sublime friction increased the wild intensity. It was too much sensation. Phenomenal but overwhelming. Unfamiliar sounds escaped her, echoing her conflicting response. She both wanted more but couldn't take it.

Maybe if she controlled the pace. She whispered, "Can I be on top?"

Had she actually said those words? She'd *never* volunteered for that position. And for good reason. It put her in charge of a situation she wasn't confident enough to control.

"Absolutely," Angelo said. His eyes flashed with dark decadence.

Yes, she could do this. Seeing him respond to her with that look —she'd take on any sexual challenge.

He rolled off her and onto his back. The sudden absence of him made her ache, and she almost whimpered. She straddled his hips, and he guided himself back inside her.

Catherine exhaled when they were connected once again and moved on top of him in a slow circle. He murmured his approval and cupped her breasts. As he rubbed his thumbs over her sensitive nipples, she dropped her head back and let out a soft sigh. It was impossible to think of how awkward she might be with the way he dominated all her senses. Instead, she focused on what her body wanted. Angelo.

"So fuckin good," he murmured in a low, delicious tone.

She slid over him, varying her pace and movements until she discovered what she liked. Circling her hips, she discovered a delicious friction that made them both moan in pleasure. He grasped her hips and thrust against her from below, and the intensity rocketed. Her panting turned into soft cries. She was desperate to reach that edge yet terrified of losing herself.

Then she gave in. She soared to that precipice and fell over, relinquishing all control. Her body exploded like it was combustible. Oh, what exquisite pleasure. She floated back to the earth in a dreamlike state as light as confetti. Each piece of her body seemed to be branded by Angelo's touch.

And why not? He'd been branded on her heart for a long time.

CHAPTER EIGHT

CATHERINE

Catherine woke the next morning when the sunlight filtered through her shades and warmed her face. An arm draped over her from behind, bringing back images of the night before.

Wow. That meant it hadn't been a wild fantasy. Angelo DeMarchis was in her bed.

After she glanced at her alarm clock, she snuggled back against him. The heat from his body and the comfort of being near him left her reluctant to get out of bed. She had twenty minutes before she had to get up for work, but the cats would be clawing at the door any minute, begging for food. Usually, they slept in the room with her, but she'd closed the door last night to avoid any little furry interruptions. For several minutes, she savored the sensation, noting each area where their bodies touched.

Had that really been her last night? She'd crawled out of her comfort zone for their one night together. In the past, when a lover would ask her to climb on top, she'd felt awkward and self-conscious. Yet what had she done last night? *Volunteered.* She couldn't bear to walk away from him with any regrets this time. Damn, that climax had made it all worth it. She'd never lost herself in passion like that before and would gladly sign up for a night like that again.

She doubted it would be the same with a different partner. The primary reason for such excitement last night wasn't the how but the who. With Angelo, every position was likely just as exhilarating.

She'd told herself it was for one night, but it couldn't be over already, could it?

Angelo stirred behind her, stretching his limbs. He pressed his body against hers, leaving no doubt that he was erect. She wiggled her ass against him, signaling she was awake and ready to play. After last night, she'd volunteer for a repeat round.

And another...

"You're awake," he murmured.

"I am. And you seem to be as well."

He chuckled. "Some parts more than others." He caressed her side and kissed the back of her neck. "I'm sure I can find a way to wake the rest of me. And have you leave this bed with a smile."

He trailed his fingers up to her breasts and fondled them, coaxing her nipples into tight peaks.

She let out a breathy sigh. "I think I still have one on my face from last night."

He nibbled her shoulder. "How much time do I have with you this morning?"

She resisted groaning as the reality of a workday intruded. "I need to get up for work in about fifteen minutes."

Moving his hand in between her legs, he stroked her. "Enough time to make you come."

Her morning routine typically consisted of a Sudoku puzzle while she waited for coffee to brew. Starting the day with the soothing consistency of numbers.

"Ooh." The familiar desire from last night returned as her body tingled. She reached back and ran her fingers along the length of his erection. "I can't think of a better way to start a Monday."

ANGELO

After a morning quickie and then a quicker breakfast, Angelo walked with Cate outside her place. She'd put on her black-framed glasses and dressed conservatively in gray slacks and a white button-down blouse with a yellow scarf. Her armor was back in place, shielding the woman who'd softened in his arms last night. He pictured running his fingers over the tiny white buttons later and unbuttoning them.

Restraining himself from acting on it now, he gave her a kiss goodbye on her lips. "I'll give you a call."

"Hope so." She smiled and climbed into her dark green Prius. As she drove away, she waved. He watched until she was out of sight and then turned to stroll through her complex. He'd called Vince to ask for a ride back to Newport and he was on the way.

The brick townhouses were built on two levels, attached on each side. A gate near the front office led to a courtyard in the middle of the residences. The SEAL in him noted how secure it was. The gate appeared to be unlocked. Hmm, he didn't like that. Anyone could stroll in there. It had a lock, though. Perhaps they locked it at night.

He turned, and his gaze shifted up to her bedroom window. What a delicious turn of events. He grinned as he thought of last night.

And this morning.

Her breathy sighs. Her delicious scent. The taste of her. And the way she wrapped herself so tightly around him. Hell, he wouldn't forget it anytime soon.

Something about being with her was different from a quick hookup. It was Cate. If she wanted him as a sex toy while he was around, he'd be the genie to grant her wish.

Damn it, he should have offered to take her out to dinner tonight.

No. It was better to keep things casual.

"Come on, come on. We're going to hit rush hour traffic!"

Angelo followed the direction of his brother's voice. Vince had pulled into the parking lot in their father's SUV. Vince circled his hand for emphasis in a perfect gruff imitation of their father.

Angelo walked down the walkway toward the car. "Do you have his knack for outwitting traffic too?"

Their dad often took twists and turns off the main roads, ending up lost in neighborhoods, as he tried to find a way to avoid being stuck at red lights.

"No, a better one." Vince raised his smartphone, displaying a navigation app. "Technology."

Angelo climbed into the car. "Thanks for picking me up."

Vince glanced at Cate's townhouse before he drove. "Looks like she's doing good for herself."

"Yes."

Vince arched his brows. "Nice bedroom?"

Angelo shook his head. "I'm not telling you shit."

"Oh, I know why you're keeping it to yourself." Vince said in a knowing tone and nodded. "You like her."

"What are you, twelve?" Angelo scoffed. "Of course I like her."

"No, I mean you're really into her."

Angelo leaned back, revealing nothing.

Vince said, "I don't need the schoolgirl jabber anyway." He turned up the volume. "I was listening to a podcast."

"On what?"

"Geek stuff. They talk about video games, sci-fi, shit I like."

Angelo leaned back in the seat while Vince drove, grateful that he'd dropped it. Angelo listened for a few minutes as two guys yammered on about their love of a new video game. Vince nodded or made sounds of acknowledgment like he was part of the discussion. Angelo grinned and then let his thoughts drift to Cate.

The last two nights had been amazing—and confusing. Buried feelings had trickled to the surface, bringing him back to a time when he was younger and more naïve. Gung-ho about heading into the military. Before he'd had his ass handed to him a dozen times before breakfast. Before multiple deployments and having to cope with death and dismemberment...

Liked her? Yes, that was one way of putting it.

They passed over the bridge above Narragansett Bay, leading to Aquidneck Island. Vince drove through Newport and turned onto a side street with modest homes where many families stationed at the naval base lived. Angelo spotted his parents' white Cape with black shutters and an American flag.

Once they entered the house, Matty looked up from his phone. "Took you long enough."

"I was in Providence," Angelo said.

"We're off to a late start," his father called from the kitchen. "But I made lunch." He raised a bagged sandwich and smiled in triumph. "Roast beef grinders with fresh meat from the deli."

"Nice." Angelo stepped into the kitchen.

His father had taught Angelo to cook, and he loved it. He couldn't often do so while on deployments, but when he had the opportunity, he enjoyed the art of creating a home-cooked meal.

His mother handed him a cooler. "Make sure you eat the fruit. Oh, and don't forget to drink water. You'll be under the sun and need to stay hydrated."

His father kissed her before leaving. "We'll be back before dinner."

Funny, despite his father's usual gruff manner, he sometimes showed a more tender side when it came to his mother.

An hour later, his father sliced through the waves on his beloved sailboat, the sea winds rippling the sail. Vince reached into the cooler and handed out cans of cold beer.

His father steered at the helm. "Nothing like it, is there?"

Matty popped the top and raised his beer. "Better than the damn desert, or some cold ass training location, that's for sure."

Vince clinked the can with his own. "Agreed."

Angelo grunted in acknowledgment and took a gulp of the cold beer. While they chattered about sailing, he stared out to the horizon. Seagulls flew in a flock, seemingly without a care. This was how he'd planned to spend leave—low-key R&R with the sea wind on his face and the salty mist spraying his skin. The sea scent wrapped around him like a shawl and he tasted it on his tongue.

Running into Cate had changed things. He wanted to see her again. How could he not after last night?

"You're quiet, Doc," Matty interrupted.

Angelo faced Matty, snapping out of his thoughts. "Just thinking."

"About Cate?" Vince said.

Did Angelo have some sappy expression on his face or something? "Why do you think that?"

His brothers exchanged a glance. Matty faced Angelo. "You gonna spill about what happened last night, or what?"

His night with Cate was off-limits. "Or what." He grinned and took another sip.

"Oh, man. You're not going to turn into one of those bonehead stories about a military dude on leave, are you? Falling for someone hard, and then doing something stupid like running off to Vegas to get married?"

Angelo scoffed. "Please, Matty. You know I have zero plans for a relationship while I'm in. What woman would put up with the bullshit of me being deployed more than I'm at home?"

"A great one," his father barked from the helm. "Like your mother."

"And it was tough on her." Tough on them all. Angelo uttered the words before he could hold them back. As the eldest, he knew first-hand how much. She'd faced numerous difficulties raising three sons. It wasn't fair to put someone through that.

Some of his father's responsibilities had fallen on Angelo. The long separations were tough on their family. The physical separation turned into a marital one. Angelo had feared his parents would divorce.

"I know." His father glanced back over his shoulder from the helm. "She's my anchor. I couldn't have made it all these years without her."

Appreciation slipped into his father's voice. Somehow, they had made their marriage work. After their trial separation, things had changed. They argued less and seemed happier. Maybe because despite the challenges, they'd committed to each other and making it work.

Was that how the guys who had a wife and family did it? They had someone to return to, someone to calm them. Someone who meant home.

With all the uncertainties in Angelo's future, was he being a fool to push away the idea of an anchor?

CATHERINE

Catherine basked in the glow of her night with Angelo. She smiled and waved as she passed coworkers on campus. The sun shone bright over the ivy-covered brick buildings, green grass, and colorful summer gardens filed with annuals. She picked up a coffee at the small café on the lower level of the building where her office was housed and then climbed up the stairs to the third floor.

She spotted her co-workers in the neuroscience department reminding her what she had to take care of this morning. After brief exchanges about the weekend, she slipped in her question, trying not to sound spooked.

"Were any of you contacted on social media this weekend by that guy Trent, the one who wrote about his memory problems?"

They hadn't.

"He contacted you?" her supervisor asked. "What did he say?"

She shrugged, trying to shake off the discomfited feeling. "More of the same. Seeing if I'd read the letter and that he was waiting for my reply."

"Don't do it," he reiterated. "And try not to take it personally. People will find some way to complain about your work. But you should report it to Security."

"Right." She tried to sound confident and not like a nervous newbie.

She returned to Frank's office and reported what had happened. He asked her to email screenshots and a link to the profile Trent used to communicate with her.

Catherine returned to her office and took care of that, and then turned to work. Focused on work, she put the incident out of her mind. Flashes of her night with Angelo returned many times throughout the morning. What was he doing? He said he'd be spending the day with his family. Would she cross his mind at all? Or was she simply another woman in his carousel?

With her lab work, supervising her interns on medical technology and brain scans, and then attending meetings with colleagues, the day rushed by. With it being summer, she wasn't teaching any classes and could spend more time on her research projects and read up on the latest findings on brain studies. That was what she loved about her job, no two days were alike. It had the structure that appealed to her yet enough variety to keep her interested and engaged.

After work, she skipped her usual spin class and instead tried a Latin dance one, feeling like trying something a little sexier than her norm. It took her a few minutes to loosen up, but she soon got into the flow. While she moved her body to the rhythm, she couldn't help but think about how Angelo had touched her.

On the drive home, she stopped at a red light. She rubbed her fingers over her lips, remembering how they'd kissed.

The person behind her honked, snapping her out of her memory. The light had turned green. Shit. She gunned forward with more acceleration than she'd meant.

He said he'd call. And she damn well hoped he did. But she wasn't going to sit around, staring at her phone, waiting for that to happen.

Back at her place, she fed the kittens and rinsed off quickly in the shower. She made herself a quick stir fry for dinner and folded laundry while watching a Ted Talk. The wild and exciting life of Catherine Boudreaux.

Two hours later, her phone flashed Angelo's name. She stared, fully confused. What about the three-day rule and all that exhausting nonsense?

Perhaps a SEAL on a short leave didn't play those foolish games.

Her heart pounded. *Stop staring and pick up the phone!*

"Hi, Angelo." Yikes, her voice came out with breathless excitement.

"Hey, Cate. Did I catch you on the run?"

"I was—uh—never mind. How are you?"

"Good. Thinking about you."

Her heart somersaulted. "Oh." Really, that's all she was going to respond? She shook her head. "What did you do today?"

"Went sailing with the family. Ate a huge meal with them. Exactly how I hoped to spend leave."

"That's nice."

"Are you free for dinner tomorrow?"

Delightful shivers ran through her. Of course, she would be available for it. Tomorrow was Tuesday. Hardly different from Monday, just a different gym class to spice up her Monday through Thursday routine–campus gym, dinner, clean up to a podcast, and then reading or watching a crime show before bed. Dinner with Angelo with the possibility of hot sex following it added some spice to her bland calendar.

Yet, she couldn't sound too eager. "I think so."

"Good. How about I meet you at your place tomorrow? Seven good?"

Her heart pumped wildly. She stifled the urge to spin through her living room like a ballerina. Keeping her voice steady, she replied, "Seven is perfect."

"Don't worry about anything. I'll pick up dinner and wine and bring it over."

She smiled at the considerate gesture. "That sounds wonderful. But, how are you going to get here?"

"I'll see if I can borrow a car."

Once she ended the call, she squealed and pounded her feet. The cats ran in, curious about the excitement.

"I have a date tomorrow!" It was un-Catherine-like behavior.

And it felt damn good.

CATHERINE ALL BUT BOLTED OUT OF BED THE NEXT MORNING, thrilled about her date with Angelo that evening. She made the bed, as she did every morning, but ensured it appeared warm and inviting with the soft bedding and extra overstuffed white pillows.

Would he take her in his arms with a heated kiss when he arrived? God, she was jittery with anticipation.

Catherine stared at the clock, counting down the hours until she met up with Angelo.

It was finally time to leave. She rushed back home and took a shower. As she lathered up, she ran her hands over her body, reliving the sensations of Angelo's hands on her.

She wavered over what to wear, something she didn't often do. She decided on a royal blue Hawaiian sundress with large orchids. It made her feel feminine. Maybe she should buy some lingerie. The idea of wearing something special for him, witnessing how it might turn him on, was a thrilling idea. But when would they have the opportunity? Time was short. She put in her contacts and applied some light makeup.

The doorbell rang. Flutters of anticipation rushed through her. She bounded down the stairs, as excited as the kittens who beat her to the front door.

Get a grip. You've known him for ten years. You shouldn't let yourself get too excited about this.

She inhaled and opened the door. Seeing him there wearing a wide smile sent giddy tremors vaulting through her. With his black shorts and forest green button-down shirt, he looked casual, yet scrumptious. The shirt brought out some green in his brown eyes. He had a paper bag in one arm, and the scent of seafood reached her.

His gaze raked over her. "You look beautiful. Hot."

The way he looked at her convinced her it was true. She returned his bold look with a flirtatious smile. "You don't look half bad yourself." She stepped aside and welcomed him in.

"Hope you're in the mood for seafood." He stepped into the kitchen. "Can't get it often when I'm deployed."

"Well then, you should have it as often as you like while you're on leave."

He planted a kiss on her lips. Although it started out like a welcoming kiss, it soon turned into something more. He pulled away for a moment to drop the paper bag on the counter and then pulled her into his arms for a deeper embrace. All the anticipation that had been building up unleashed a heady wave of passion within her. She grasped for him like she needed him to breathe. While he did the same, claiming her body everywhere he could touch.

He pulled back and stared down at her. "Funny, I'm no longer hungry—for dinner at least."

"Oh?" She arched an eyebrow. "And what are you hungry for?"

"I should think that's obvious." Angelo gave her a dark, decadent look that left little guessing to what was on his mind. "I've been thinking about you all day. And I couldn't wait to get back here to see you."

Those words thrilled her more than they should. Getting so excited about a fleeting encounter was silly.

Then again, why shouldn't she enjoy herself for once? Why did it have to mean anything more than what it was? Surely, it didn't to him. He might have women tucked away in many corners of the world. She needed to get over herself with thinking this might mean something to him. It was better to enjoy their time together for what it was meant to be—a fling and nothing more.

"I hope you do more than just see me." She wrapped her hands around the back of his neck and rose to kiss him.

His hands trailed down her body, claiming her. She moved her hands down over the strong muscles in his back, down to his waist, over his ass.

He pressed his hard length against her and moaned. "God, Cate, you're killing me. I want you so bad."

They stumbled through her place and into her living room, almost knocking down a lamp, before he ended up on top of her on the couch. She tore at his clothes, frantic to shed the obstacles between them. She had to get closer to him. Needed the skin to skin contact.

Needed him.

Soon, their clothes lay in a pile on the floor. She reached over and closed the window so no one would hear them. They kissed as they ground their naked bodies together. An echo of the salty ocean scent lingered on his skin. She breathed it in.

He moved down to kiss her breasts and she moaned. God, he was so good at drawing out her pleasure. She trailed her fingers through his hair. When he stroked between her legs, heat spread throughout her body, igniting a deeper yearning. She needed him inside her.

"Angelo, now. Please."

He pulled his head up and gave her a smoldering look. "Please what?" His voice dropped to a low seductive tone.

"You know. I want you."

"Want me how?"

Oh no, he was going to tease her, wasn't he?

"I want to hear you say it."

"Why?" She gasped.

"It turns me on."

"Okay," She convinced herself to say the words. "Fuck me, Angelo. Please."

Words she'd never said sounded foreign from her mouth. And oh so naughty.

His grin was victorious. "Yesss."

He pulled himself away to put on a condom and then he slid against her folds. She grabbed his shoulder blades, coaxing him in. As he filled her, she sighed. He was what she craved. She clung to him as she allowed herself to be swept away. The reality might not last, but it would fuel her fantasies for a long time.

CHAPTER NINE

ANGELO

They rolled off her couch and onto the brown carpet with swirly designs. Angelo knelt behind her and reached around to caress her breasts. He nuzzled her neck and kissed her sweet-smelling skin. Already missing the sensation of being inside her, he ached to bury himself again.

He pressed his chest against her back and stroked down the front of her body, seeking that sweet spot between her legs. So hot.

"You feel so good. So wet."

She moaned and leaned against him. "I want you."

He rubbed his cock at her slick entrance, and she fell forward, using her arms to brace herself. She turned back over her shoulder and bit her lip. Nervous?

"Are you okay like this?"

After a moment's hesitation, she smiled. "Yes."

He gripped her hips and slid in. Although he started slow, he couldn't resist driving into her this way. Once fully in, he dropped his head back as he reveled in the sensation.

She felt too damn good as he took her from behind. The rug burn on their knees might be a bitch later, but it was worth it. Her passionate sounds filled his ears. And the rough, primal way their bodies joined fueled the excitement.

He wouldn't last long at this rate, but he damn well wouldn't come until she did. Preferably multiple times.

It took all his reserves to slow down and not fuck her the way he wanted. He reached forward and thumbed her nipples, finding this new distraction utterly pleasurable. Was it pleasurable for her as well? He slid his fingers over her stomach and down between her legs. She gasped, but then pressed against him. He stroked her, teasing her sensitive nub and she moaned.

As her breathy moans escalated so did his excitement. Their pace quickened again as he pumped into her harder. He steeled himself to hold on a little longer, applying more pressure.

With a cry, her body tightened, and she shattered. Her slick channel pulsed around him, squeezing his shaft. He couldn't hold back any longer. He grasped her hips and dropped his head back as he released himself inside of her, letting out a low groan. He lost sense of time and place as he willingly drowned in this delicious ecstasy.

A thousand degrees hotter, covered in a sheen of perspiration, Angelo draped one arm across her. They lay together on the rug, and their breathing still came quick. After thinking about her all day, and finally getting close to her again, he didn't want to let her go just yet.

ANGELO

When his breathing level normalized and he could speak, he said, "Sorry, I didn't mean to go all caveman on you and jump on you the second I walked through the door."

Cate gave him a sassy look. "And what gave you the impression that you need to apologize? I thought I exhibited my enjoyment."

"Yes, you did seem to express some pleasure." He winked.

"I'm not usually like that. So, um, bold. You know, in that position and all. Or, uh, vocal."

Angelo smiled with self-satisfaction. "Happy to bring out that side of you."

He leaned in to take a deeper inhale of the scent of her hair. Some sort of citrus fragrance, like orange blossoms. He wanted to remember her scent. Hell, he wanted to remember her taste, her touch, everything about her.

Fuck. This wasn't good. Committing her to memory like this would make it more difficult to leave. He'd seen the other guys moon about missing their wives and girlfriends, but he couldn't afford that mental taxation. He was a SEAL. His team relied on him to take care of them. He couldn't be distracted, pining over a woman who could be thousands of miles away.

Yet, plenty of SEALs were married.

If the other guys could do it, maybe it came down to a personal decision.

"Did you just smell my hair?" she asked.

Busted. "No," he lied. "What if I had been?"

"I'd say you're strange." She laughed. "It's just shampoo and conditioner."

Hell no, it wasn't just something from a bottle. It was more. It was Cate. Not that he would tell her that.

"Come on let's eat." He gave her a playful swat on her ass. "I'm starving."

He went into her bathroom to clean up. After dressing, he stared at himself in the mirror. The last face that Donovan saw. Angelo gritted his teeth. Would that reminder ever go away? He doubted it. But maybe one day it wouldn't stab him like a blade.

He splashed water over his face. "Don't let your head get in the way and ruin this," he told his reflection. Then he returned to her kitchen and reheated the seafood.

The kitchen had to be 800 degrees. "It's so hot in here."

She poured them glasses of Pinot Grigio. "Well, yes. We kind of heated things up."

"Don't you have A/C?"

"Sure, I have central air, but I like having the windows open. Getting some natural air in here."

He raised his eyebrows. "You call city air natural?"

She laughed. "It's better than being cooped up with all the windows closed."

He pulled out plates from her cabinet. "You might not be saying that if you spend months over in the desert, sweating in 100+ degrees."

She gestured in his direction. "Fine. While you're here, we'll put on central air. Happy?"

He grinned at her. "More than you know."

Once she turned on the air, they sat at her dining room table to eat.

He ate a clam strip. "Anything fun and exciting happen at work today?"

She finished chewing a bite of cod. "I spent a good part of the day having one-on-ones with my summer interns."

"Doing what?"

"They're helping in the lab—examining brain imagery, entering data, and so on."

"Sounds interesting."

She shrugged. "To me, it is. Not sure if it would intrigue anyone else. I spend much of my time in the brain lab, supervising interns, working on my computer, or attending meetings."

The slightly higher tone in her voice indicated something was up. Her expression darkened. What the hell was it with her work? He was used to studying people and keyed in to signals of deceit. She didn't want to tell him for whatever reason. Fine. He didn't blame her. She had no reason to trust him.

But it would be nice if she did.

What was wrong with him? He shouldn't care. Time to change the topic. "Was MIT as tough as I hear?"

Her eyes lit up. "It was tough, yes, but I loved it. The workload was stressful. Just about everyone feels imposter syndrome there at one point or another. But once I graduated, I felt a real sense of accomplishment. Know what I mean?"

He nodded. "I do. Going through BUD/S was hell. But then, once I survived it—no greater victory."

"What is BUD/S?"

"The intense training to become a SEAL."

"Oh, I really don't know much about the military. Let alone SEALs." She shook her head, gesturing as if flustered. "What you went through must have been hell. I can't even imagine it. It makes my academic challenges look trivial in comparison."

"Not at all. I'd never think that. It took a lot of guts and hard work and sacrifices to get where you are. I respect that immensely."

Her lips twitched as if undecided if she should smile at his praise.

"But I know what you mean," he added. "When you face a challenge, you question why you're doing it and if you can handle it. When you push yourself through and finally reach your goal, there's nothing like it. Makes it all worth it in the end. It's not all physical, what SEALs face. Many barriers are in your head." He tapped his skull for emphasis.

The way she gazed at him with near fascination almost leveled him.

"Tell me about where you've been. What you've done," she said.

"I spent much of the first couple of years in training. It was intense but necessary. The harder we're trained, the better prepared we are. And then once I was assigned to a team, the fun has never stopped." He gave her a lopsided grin.

Talking to her felt good, but he wanted to touch her too. She was too far away, across the table, and all he could think about were all the ways he wanted to do just that.

Somehow, he made it through dinner without throwing her on the table and taking her right there. Why was he responding to her like this, like he was a teenager and could barely keep it in his pants? Was it because that's what it was like when they were younger? Shit, it was no small feat to keep from touching her again. Her silky hair. Her soft skin.

As they cleaned the dishes, he couldn't resist any longer. He stepped behind her and kissed the delicate skin on the back of her neck. Her taste, her unique scent. It was addictive.

When she moaned, it fed his addiction. He moved his hands down to cup her breasts. Fuck, she'd gotten him so hard again already.

He rubbed his bulge against her ass. "Look what you've done to me."

She arched against him and moved her hips, shooting his desire up to aching levels.

"I can't say I'm sorry for doing that." She arched one brow. "In fact, I'm quite happy about this response. It's Pavlovian, in a way. I wiggle my butt against you, and I get rewarded."

He laughed and gave her ass a playful slap. "Bed."

"You don't want a reboot? On the sofa?" she teased.

"Not right now. I want all the play space we can find."

"Do you plan on—*playing* in there?"

"Affirmative, ma'am," he replied in a playful tone.

They hurried up the stairs. Once in her room, he backed her onto the bed. Sliding his body over hers, he kissed her neck, savoring her scent. "I couldn't choose a better—playmate."

CHAPTER TEN

CATHERINE

The next morning, Angelo made coffee and blueberry pancakes.

"You're spoiling me." After she took a sip of the delicious hazelnut brew, she asked, "What do you have planned today?"

"The usual. Hang out with my family. Maybe get a workout in with my brothers. Then, if you're up for it, come back here to spoil you with my cooking and sexual prowess."

She laughed. He had been spoiling her with both indeed. "That sounds like a great idea to me."

They each ate some more pancakes.

"What about you," Angelo asked. "What's going on at work today?"

"Good question. Let me check my schedule." She pulled out her phone to check her calendar. The usual project meetings with her team. She flipped to her email app to make sure nothing else had come up.

One was addressed from a sender reading "brain research." She couldn't resist an inquiry like that. She opened it and regret swamped her.

It was from Trent.

He likely created another throwaway email account since the other one had been blocked by IT.

I'm getting impatient...

That's all it read.

Why? A dark shiver ran along her spine.

"Cate? What's wrong?" Angelo asked.

She shook her head. "Oh, it's nothing. Work stuff."

"You turned white and froze. You look terrified."

Shit. She'd never play against him in poker. He'd read everything on her face.

He dropped his fork and leaned back in his chair. "Is someone bothering you?"

Cate squirmed under the scrutiny. "Not exactly."

"Well, what exactly?"

"It is—sort of—a nuisance."

"What is?"

She took a deep breath. "A man has contacted me a few times."

Angelo straightened, his expression turned grave. "What man? And how?"

"It's just some guy who has been contacting my team to warn us about our research for the government."

"Warning you how? Is he threatening you?" His voice lowered with a dangerous edge, as if she'd woken up the warrior and set him on full alert.

He wouldn't relent until he knew all the answers, would he? "No. He is warning researchers who work on government contracts. He said they have messed with his memory. Most of what he writes doesn't make sense. Words strung together without much meaning. He needs help." She paused, gauging what else to reveal. "He addressed his letters to me as Miss Catherine Boudreaux in tiny, capitalized letters. Not doctor and not Ms., which is odd—like he knows I'm not married." Once she started talking about this situation she'd tried to minimize, her worries spilled out.

"That's why I had that idea the night of the wedding," she continued. "He contacted me on social media, and it was fresh in my mind. It rattled me—and when you didn't recognize me—well, I guess I carried it over to make you uncomfortable as well." She gave him a sheepish expression. "It wasn't my best moment."

Angelo leaned back in the chair, keeping his posture straight. He eyed Cate for a long moment and then asked, "Have you reported this to anyone?"

"Yes. I told the security team at the university."

"What have they done?" Suspicion rose in his tone.

Her jaw twitched. "They said they'll look into it."

Angelo grunted. "Have you asked them for updates?"

ANGELO

She exhaled. "They're not going to give me the details of an ongoing investigation, are they?"

"It depends on the circumstances. You could ask."

"I can't overreact." She gestured with a wave. "It's not like I'm the only person on my team who has been contacted. It sounds to me like a cry for help. When I mentioned to security how we should suggest options, they told me not to respond and they'd take care of it, and if I reached out, it would encourage him to continue the conversation."

Angelo's expression revealed nothing. He gripped his mug like squeezing a fist. "What about the local police?"

"What about them?"

"You haven't got them involved?"

"Why would I?" She raised her hand to her temple. "The university is already involved. I'm working on a government-funded project—of course it's going to be controversial on some level. You can't even post a comment online anymore without people going rabid, making some sort of political statement, and then eight thousand people jumping in to attack with their opinions."

He snorted. "You're absolutely right there." He studied her and cocked his head. "Do you feel threatened?"

She shifted in her chair. "It's not like he's singling me out or anything." She rolled her shoulders back as if spiders had suddenly fallen onto them and were crawling toward her neck. "Except for social media. I'm the only one he's contacted that way so far."

Angelo scrutinized her. "This guy sounds like a stalker."

Whoa, maybe she shouldn't have told him. "Angelo, you're blowing this out of proportion."

His mouth tightened with a grim line. "I don't like it. You should go to the police."

"No." She waved her hands to the sides. "If I want to be treated like a professional, I need to act like one. This is my first time as a project lead at the university."

He narrowed eyes. "I don't follow."

"Being a woman in STEM is already difficult. If I run to the police when the security team is already taking care of the situation, I come off as terrified and weak. It undermines my team's confidence in my abilities. It's hard enough to establish a reputation in academia and I need to project myself as capable—not timid."

Angelo said nothing. He stabbed a bit of pancakes and appeared thoughtful as he chewed. After he swallowed, he said, "If you give people the benefit of the doubt, they'll take advantage."

She raised her eyebrows at that. What was he saying? That she was naïve? "I'm not a SEAL, but that doesn't mean I'm some clueless woman bumbling around in the world. I have managed to take care of myself for a long time."

He leaned forward. "I didn't say you were clueless, Cate, but this situation could be dangerous. Don't you see it? If you're not going to get the police involved, then I want to."

She'd picked up a piece of pancake with her fork and paused, syrup dripping from the end. "What?"

"I want to stay here make sure you're okay."

She blinked a few times and lowered her fork. "You *have* been staying here."

"Yes. But this is different." His expression turned hard, determined. "I'm not going to let some whack job get to you."

ANGELO

Catherine grunted and threw her hands up. "Would you stop? I've devoted my career to studying the brain. Part of that involves helping people with brain trauma and mental issues. Not labeling them with insults."

"You're right." He gritted his teeth. "I hate the idea of anyone bothering you. You've been trained one way, I have another. It's hard to let down your guard when you're trained to be alert for danger."

She nodded. "I can understand that. But you're on leave."

They stared at each other for several seconds, tension looming between them. Angelo broke the tension with a lopsided grin. "My awareness doesn't have an on/off switch."

She nodded. "Okay. But, still—you should be relaxing, not volunteering to be my bodyguard."

"What if I find guarding your body—and exploring it in many ways—the best way to spend my leave?" His tone lowered with decadent promise and his eyes twinkled with mischievousness.

Unanticipated heat tingled on her skin. "Angelo..." Her voice came out as breathless as a sigh.

He leaned back in his chair. "Are we getting somewhere? Understanding each other's point of view?"

A small grin broke through her frustration. "Perhaps."

With their different takes on the situation, formed by different experiences, what could they do to find some level ground?

Compromise. That was the way her parents solved problems. Each of them had to give way a bit, so they'd meet somewhere in the middle. It was better for both people to feel they walked away with something, rather than a winner and loser. That was no way to have a healthy relationship.

But this wasn't a relationship. It was a fling.

Then why did it feel like more?

Time to put her parent's way to the test. Instead of being stubborn and standing her ground, she posed, "Compromise?"

"Sure."

"What would make you happy in this situation?"

"Staying here. Making sure you're safe so I don't pace the floor, wondering if you're okay."

Her heart beat more quickly. He wanted to protect her. How could she not respond to that? Still, she couldn't be selfish. "What about spending time with your family?"

"I do spend time with them while you're at work." He chuckled. "Too much time, sometimes. I live with a team of guys, and now I'm with my brothers. I prefer sleeping in a bed with you rather than sleeping in a house crowded with testosterone."

Her lips quirked. "I enjoy that, too."

"I want to come back here tonight." He stood and walked over to her and then ran his index finger over her cheek and over her bottom lip. "Because I want to see you again."

She tried to stop it from trembling. Wherever he skimmed, his fingers left a trail of scorching heat.

He took her hand and she stood before him. Then he trailed his fingers over the side of her neck and collarbone, running them down to her breast and stroking a nipple with his thumb. Her body simmered, responding to his touch. The atmosphere between them had shifted, from tense to sensual.

"Is staying here still on the table?" he murmured with a brush of his lips against her ear.

She cocked a brow. "On the table. On the sofa. On the counter. Or bed…"

Angelo glanced at her with an irresistible grin. "I'm game for all of the above."

"Yes, stay." As if she'd ever want him to leave. "But only if you agree to keep things as they are."

"Meaning?"

"No bodyguard kind of stuff, like stalking through the bushes or peering out windows for danger, or any GI Joe stuff."

"SEAL stuff," he corrected.

"Fine, no crazy SEAL stunts."

"Okay, so what do you want?"

For him to be there because he wanted to be, not because he felt some duty to protect her. "The way things have been. Dinner. Sex. Lots of sex." She cocked her head and smiled. "And delicious breakfasts the morning after."

"I'm already getting hungry." His voice dropped to a deliciously dark tone. He ran his finger over her bottom lip. "Are you getting hungry, Cate?"

He stepped closer and bent down, brushing his lips against her throat.

Heat coiled through her body. Her breath came quicker. "Yes."

"Looks like I received new orders," he murmured.

She blinked. "What?"

"Relocate to your bed."

She laughed. "Yes. I have another hour or so before I have to leave."

They hurried upstairs and he lowered her onto the bed. The dark glint in his eyes made her pulse quicken. Damn, he was breathtaking. Why did their time together have to be so short?

The answer came clear from a dark recess in her mind. Because if he stayed in town much longer, she might be in danger of falling in love with him.

She was halfway there already.

Angelo lowered himself onto her and silenced her thoughts with a deep kiss. Heat reignited deep inside her. She wrapped her arms around him, ruffling her fingers over the shorter hair at the base of his neck.

"Oh, Angelo," she murmured.

"I'm right here." He moved his mouth to her neck and then gave her a gentle bite on her shoulder. "And here." Then he moved down to her breast and further down.

She sucked in a breath, anticipating his next move.

He kissed below her belly button. "And here…"

CHAPTER ELEVEN

ANGELO

After Angelo returned to Newport, he and his brothers headed to the football stadium. He tightened the laces of his sneakers at the foot of the bleachers. Once he stood, he scanned the route around the stands. They should have come earlier in the morning. The near noontime sun gleamed down on them. At least working out with his brothers would help him get out of his head for a while, and not fixate on those messages sent to Cate. She might have thought he was overreacting, but it was always better to be prepared.

Matty pulled his Red Sox hat lower, blocking more of the sun. He wore his usual workout shorts. Today it was black and paired with a red compression shirt.

"You look worried. You sure you can handle this, old man?" he teased.

Angelo huffed. "You sure you have enough experience, little brother?"

Vince chuckled and ran his hand over his stubble like it was a foreign object. He'd taken a break from the clean-cut shave demanded in the Marines but wore a Semper Fi T-shirt announcing his affiliation.

"What are you laughing at, Devil Dog?" Matty turned to Vince. "I bet you don't even make it to section five."

Vince put on aviator sunglasses and then alternated legs as he stretched in a lunging position up the bleachers. "So much talk, man, and such little action."

"Is that right?" Matty faced forward. "3-2-1-Go!" He bolted up the steps.

Vince swore under his breath and followed. Angelo shook his head. Jackasses. They'd burn out in no time at that rate. He went through some dynamic stretches and then ran up the first stairs, using a slower pace to ease into the workout. In each section, he altered his pace and technique. He ran quicker up the stairs and took longer, slower lunging steps up the bleachers.

He caught up with his brothers about a third of the way through the sections. Both sat and panted. They'd taken off their T-shirts and glistened with sweat.

Angelo laughed. "You rocks. Would you start out a marathon with a sprint?"

Matty wiped sweat from his forehead with his shirt. "It's hot as fuck out here. That's why."

"Please," Angelo countered. "We're not in the desert. It's just that you're competitive as fuck."

Vince turned to Matty, reflecting a miniature version of him in his mirrored sunglasses. "Trying to prove you're as tough as your big brothers."

"Bullshit," Matty barked under a fake cough. "I'm still in my peak, while you're both pushing past your prime."

Vince shook his head and laughed. "I'm with you this time, man." He raised his chin at Angelo. "Instead of shit-for-brains." He pointed his thumb at Matty.

"You're not ditching me," Matty said. "I'm coming."

"Drink more water so you don't get dehydrated," Angelo directed. "I don't want to have to carry either of you back because you passed out."

"Yes, Doc," Matty acknowledged with a sly grin.

Angelo removed his T-shirt as well as it had started clinging to him. With the sun beating down and his body heating up, the fewer clothes, the better. After a few more minutes, Angelo led his brothers at his pace and technique. They caught the eyes of some college girls also working out in the stadium.

"Looking good, ladies," Matty acknowledged.

He didn't abandon the workout to go flirt but followed Angelo's directions breaking up the workout with rounds of pushups and squat-thrusts. They finished the stairs, and then cooled down with a lap around the nearby track.

Matty prodded Vince. "We should go talk to them when we're done."

"Yeah, you smell great," Vince replied in his wry tone.

Matty sniffed. "I've smelled worse. And so have you." He nodded. "They might find it manly."

"Oh yeah, irresistible," Vince quipped.

Angelo ignored them. He didn't have any interest in the women. Only one was on his mind. The situation with Cate returned. What would his brothers think? They wouldn't hold back if they thought Angelo was overreacting and acting like some possessive caveman.

"I want to run something by you both."

"Shoot," Vince said.

"This guy has been contacting Cate," he began, unable to keep the tension from his tone.

"Is there an *and* or a *but* coming?" Matty asked.

Angelo pulled at his beard. "Yes. *And* he's been warning her and some co-workers about their work for the government. Some nut claiming the government has messed with his memories."

Vince's expression turned grim. "Has he made threats?"

"Not that I know. But I haven't read the messages. It sounds like a rant about what happened to his memory."

Matty snapped his fingers. "Sounds like someone wrapped up in conspiracy theories."

That's what Angelo thought and couldn't stop thinking about. He didn't mention it again until they'd finished the lap and headed onto the grass to cool down.

He lunged forward to stretch out his legs. "Cate reported it at the university, and supposedly they're looking into it. She hasn't told the local police. I think she should, but she thinks I'm over-reacting. Am I?"

Vince rolled his shoulders back and pulled one arm across his chest. "It depends. If it's just a mass mailing, it's probably just spam. But, if it's more targeted at Cate—with a specific threat—then I'd be concerned."

Angelo nodded and stretched out the other leg. Perhaps Vince was right. Still, he didn't like anyone bothering Cate, in any way. If he could stop it, he would.

"I told her if she wasn't going to have the cops watch out for her, then I'd stay there."

"That's one way to ensure the return invitation to her bed," Matty quipped.

Angelo shot Matty a look. "It's more than that. Something about this sets me on edge. I don't like it."

Vince reached behind him to hold his ankle and stretch his quad. "If you're there, you can watch for anything off, and note things she might have overlooked."

"But then what happens after you leave?" Matty cocked his head.

Angelo scowled. That was something he didn't want to think about. Sure, he was around to protect her now, but what happened next week when he was back with his team in Little Creek? And then sent to who knows where for who knew how long?

"I don't know." He gritted his teeth.

"I'm not just talking about this dude," Matty clarified. "What happens with you and Cate?"

Angelo exhaled. He took a swig of water from his stainless-steel bottle. That was another question. A big one. And one he didn't have any idea of how to answer.

"Hell, if I know."

"Doc, you seem to have your shit together," Matty said. "But then you see a girl from high school and turn as mushy as grits? I don't get it."

Ignoring Matty, Angelo sat on the grass, and stretched his legs wide. As he leaned forward, the scent of the grass filled his nose. Matty's words echoed in Angelo's head. He didn't get it either. Things had morphed quickly with Cate. Although he'd been the one who had warned he wasn't cut out for a relationship, he was also the one who had practically insisted he move in while on leave.

Hell, Cate was the one who studied brains. What would she think about the questions in his head?

Did he want to watch over her or was it something more?

THE NEXT AFTERNOON, ANGELO TRIED A DIFFERENT TACTIC TO head over to Cate's. He wanted to make the best of the summer day without a cloud in the bluebird sky. He rented a bike in Newport and rode over to East Bay Bike Path to travel to Providence. One of his favorite routes, it offered him spectacular water views. He wanted to soak in as much as he could before returning to some dry desert or dense forest. It would take a couple of hours or so to reach Cate's place, but it doubled as his workout.

Last night, he'd struggled not to come off as a paranoid SEAL on watch for danger when he'd returned to Cate's. She wanted things to remain normal and he didn't blame her. She'd called him out on it last night.

Angelo, you're doing it again.

What?

It's the third time I've seen you scan the windows like an intruder is going to burst through them.

Sorry.

Remember our deal.

Food and sex, how could I forget? Every man's dream.

He struggled to tone down his surveillance so as not to freak her out. Still, he'd remain vigilant for anything—or anyone—intrusive.

The route he rode today took him along the sea and through woodlands, which offered the respite of shade under the summer sun warming his skin. Birds sang overhead as if they didn't have a care in the world. After several miles of riding, he took a break where water surrounded the path on both sides. The more time he spent here along the shore, the more he sensed he was slowly healing. The serene natural beauty was like a balm to his battered soul. He took out his water bottle, drank, and then fortified himself with an energy bar before he continued the ride.

The end of his leave loomed ahead. Leave days zoomed by so much faster than those on deployment. Perhaps because while he was away, he was often counting down the times before he would return to the States. Like most everyone did. He was married to the SEALs as the saying went, but that didn't mean deployments were a honeymoon. Far from it. They were a shit show most of the time. Little sleep, no hot water, and the constant vigilance of knowing someone wanted you dead.

But hey, that was the life he'd chosen, and he had no regrets. He was proud to be a SEAL and grateful to have saved lives.

This leave whipped by even faster because of Cate. He enjoyed every moment with her. He couldn't wait for the weekend when they could spend more time together.

Angelo stopped in an Italian market he spotted to pick up some fresh pasta. He planned to cook chicken and eggplant parmesan with a side Caesar salad. And buy a good bottle of wine to go with it.

She'd given him a key that morning so he could get dinner started while she finished up at work. His brothers had teased him about it endlessly. Ribbing him about playing house. Perhaps that was the case, but hell, he loved to cook. Cate had a great little kitchen for cooking for two. Or a small family.

He grunted. *Don't go there.*

Right, no need to mess his head up with unrealistic ideas. He picked up his backpack and then rode the last few minutes to her apartment and let himself in. The kittens ran up to him as they did each time, meowing as if they hadn't seen him for months and were starved for affection.

"Hey girls, calm down. I'm here. I'll get you some treats." He bent down and rubbed each of their chins. They couldn't seem to get enough, rubbing their faces against his hand. When he focused on one, the other rubbed against his leg. Marking him. He laughed. "Don't get too used to me, kitties. I'm only around another week."

They'd forget him soon enough. All they wanted was the human who would provide food and treats. Maybe some affection too.

A strange sort of ache filled him. Would Cate forget him so soon, too?

Angelo rinsed the sweat off from the bike ride with a quick shower. Then he got to work in the kitchen.

He emptied the bag of groceries and washed the vegetables. He set up his workstation and timed what he needed to do to have the pasta boiled at the right time when the chicken and eggplant was ready.

While he prepped, he thought about Cate. Had this guy contacted her again? What did he want from her? Was he an actual threat or was Angelo letting his combat experiences cloud his vision?

He glanced at the clock. It was 4:15. Cate would get home after five and he wanted her to walk into her place to the smell of a delicious meal. That didn't happen often, if ever, for someone who lived alone.

Unless, she'd had other lovers who she'd given the keys to...

He growled. He'd just have to make sure his meal and presentation were unforgettable.

Angelo glanced around her kitchen for whatever else he could do to enhance the dining experience. He found an apron hanging on a hook and spread it out. It read *Warning, Mad Scientist. Explosions happen.* It gave him an idea. He could keep things lighter the way she wanted and not rattle her with his higher vigilance.

He took off his clothes in her bedroom and put on the apron. Then he returned to the kitchen with a sly smile on his face.

CATHERINE

Despite how wonderful it was to have Angelo stay at her place, his heightened awareness was like a new roommate. He searched for threats like he was a programmed surveillance system. The tension wrapped around her as well, escalating her wariness.

Maybe she shouldn't have told him.

When she reached the university, Catherine forced herself to push his concerns out of her mind. After all, nobody else was giving it a second thought.

Then again, Trent appeared to contact her more often than most—and in more ways.

At least, she had plenty to distract her. That was what she'd loved about her job. She could lose herself while studying an image of the brain, searching for clues as if piecing together a puzzle. The brain was fascinating with so much still to be discovered.

Excited about meeting up with Angelo for dinner, she left work earlier than planned. The scent of tomato sauce cooking wafted out of her kitchen window as she approached her door. Fireflies zipped about inside her, sending a fluttering sensation that rose as she turned the knob. She couldn't wait to see him again.

When she opened the door, his back faced her as he cooked over the stove. Her gaze dropped to his bare ass, and her mouth fell open. It was a fine muscular butt that made her gaze linger —but why was he wearing nothing while he cooked dinner?

"Angelo? You're naked."

He spun around with a smirk. "Not completely. Yet."

He wore an apron, her Mad Scientist one. It was a joke gift from her family after a disastrous meal she'd tried to cook them when she first bought the townhouse. The pasta and sauce had burned, the smoke detectors had gone off, and they'd ended up going out to a restaurant. A muscular Navy SEAL wearing nothing else but that. She burst out with a laugh.

He raised a cooking spoon and gave her a mock affronted look. "I cook dinner for you, and you laugh in my face?"

"You look ridiculous. And you know it. You got the exact reaction that you were going for."

"Well, not exactly." He put the spoon down on the spoon holder and approached her with a dark glimmer in his eyes. "Maybe I was hoping you'd see me half naked and wouldn't be able to resist jumping on me." He tapped the counter. "Beg me to take you right here."

That wasn't a bad idea. Especially when his seductive glance made her think of all the decadent things they could be doing—flashing back to some of those naughty things that they'd already done.

She wrapped her arms around his neck and greeted him with a kiss. "Hi. Thank you for making me dinner. It smells delicious."

"You're welcome. That's better."

She gave him a suggestive glance. "How about taking off that apron and taking me instead?"

His face spread into a broad grin. "One second." He turned off the oven and said, "Dinner can wait."

CHAPTER TWELVE

ANGELO

"Wow," Catherine murmured in between quick breaths. "I can't believe we christened the counter."

His heart still raced, and his body burned hotter than the heat in her kitchen. He lowered his forehead to touch Cate's. "That was quite the appetizer."

She murmured, "Very tasty."

He pulled himself out of her with reluctance. "I better clean up and serve dinner."

Minutes later, he served the chicken onto her crisp white dinner plates. She poured them glasses of chardonnay. He had to get a hold of himself. Whenever he was near her, he couldn't seem to greet her without his libido firing off like a rocket-propelled grenade.

They sat at her oval wood table and finally ate. Watching her enjoy the dinner he'd prepared filled his chest with warmth.

"How was work?" He kept his voice neutral to avoid triggering her wariness.

"Fine. A typical day."

"So, no contact from the guy?"

Her expression tightened with discomfort. Why had he blurted that out?

"No, Angelo." Her voice came out lower.

"Would you tell me if he did?"

What the fuck was wrong with him? Why not call her a straight up liar?

She picked up the napkin and wiped her mouth. "Don't do this." She placed her hands on her lap. "This is a wonderful meal, and I want to enjoy it with you. Not talk about that."

"Okay."

"The situation already stresses me out. When I'm with you, that's the last thing I want to think about."

His jaw tightened. "Got it."

"How was the day with your family?" she asked with a smile.

She steered the conversation back to him because she was uncomfortable about that discussion. He was picking up on her quirks and that was a Catherine Boudreaux standard.

"We ate a big lunch, we gave each other shit about stupid things, you know—our usual."

She laughed. Once they were finished, she covered her stomach. "That was delicious, Angelo. Thank you."

A strange heated tingle spread throughout him. "I'm glad you liked it."

"I'm so full. Want to head out for a walk?"

"Sure." It would be good to get out of her house where he wouldn't be tempted to take her on the couch. Or the rug. Or her bed. Or the counter—again.

"Where are we headed?" he asked.

"Just around the neighborhood. Thought we'd get outside and get some fresh air, rather than keeping you cooped up in my place your entire leave."

He grinned. "I've been quite content to be holed up with you and all your womanly wiles."

"And you and all your manly—" she glanced down at his lower body and then returned her gaze to his face with a naughty look. "—cooking."

He laughed. "Is that the only reason you enjoy having me around?" He pulled her into his arms and glanced down at her. "My cooking skills?"

She tilted her head. "You might have a few other skills I appreciate as well."

He cupped her ass and squeezed. "I might try to figure out what you appreciate about me most."

"Later." With a raised brow she added, "Definitely later." She moved out of his embrace and grabbed his hand. "Come on. Let's head out."

As they walked out of her neighborhood, he didn't release her hand. She didn't pull it away either, a good sign. Funny, he wasn't much of a hand holder. It was something he associated with old married couples, not young lovers. But Cate complicated his attempt at maintaining a distance. She was different. Like a close friend, but with killer sexual attraction.

Whatever it was, he liked it. It wasn't just comfortable, it felt right.

He scanned the environment for anything off. It was a habit to search for threats and entrance and exit routes. This residential area where she lived seemed quiet and sleepy, not dangerous like some of the urban environments he'd been in. It was full of townhouses and multi-family homes, many with pristine landscaping and gardens. But for this guy who sounded like a stalker, it provided many concealed spaces for him to hide.

All appeared quiet. Shit, he had to relax with the overprotectiveness.

They turned onto a main road full of commercial buildings and walked by numerous stores and restaurants. The mouthwatering aromas would have called to him had they not just eaten. The flashing lights of a venue with video games lured him over.

He pointed. "We *have* to go in here."

She laughed. "What are you, ten?"

"Trust me, it's fun. It's a different feel from staying in a room by yourself playing a video game, staring at your computer or TV. You get the energy from everyone around you."

"It's your time off." She gave him a smile that melted him. "You can spend it however you like."

"Nice." He wiggled his eyebrows. "I'll kick your butt in some old-school arcade games." When he playfully swatted her rear, she yelped.

"Game on," she affirmed.

Her spirited expression with a gleam in her eyes reminded him of her competitive streak in high school—academically. She didn't care about sports, but when it came to math or science competitions, she was fierce.

Catherine raised her index finger. "But no, I'm not going up against you in any shooting games." She planted her hands on her hips. "Not with a SEAL."

He laughed and put his arm around her shoulder. "I'll win you a stuffed bunny or something."

They spent the next hour navigating through people and machines, surrounded by colorful lights and the excited beeps of the arcade. Scents of buttery popcorn and fried food wafted around them. Angelo not only won her a stuffed bunny, he accumulated a roll of tickets from video games and skee ball. She earned a fair share, as well.

"Do you want these?" He held up his tickets.

"No, I don't need anything else."

He scanned the people around them looking for kids. A boy and girl who appeared to be in elementary school were counting their tickets while looking at the prizes they could redeem them for that were behind the glass counter.

"Here are some more for you to share." He offered his stash.

They stared at them as if he'd offered him a treasure box full of toys and candy. After thanking him, they gushed over their expanded prize options.

Catherine tapped his arm as they walked away from the kids. "That was nice of you. You could have claimed a few hundred Tootsie Rolls for yourself."

He flashed her a one-sided grin. "It was tough to give them up." When he spotted the air hockey table, he turned to her and said, "You have to play this with me."

She laughed. "You're like a kid in here, rather than a big, tough SEAL. It's good to see you having fun."

He arched a brow. "Maybe it's not just the arcade, but the company." It was the truth. He enjoyed spending time with her. Hell, he'd be content if they were still at her place, sitting on her couch. Sure, he'd probably find another way to play with her, most likely slipping his hands under her shirt and in between her legs.

"Hold on, let me give my tickets away too," she said. "Where's a kid who doesn't have any?"

As she scanned the kids, he watched her. That was thoughtful for her to think that way. Sure, maybe a part of him had been trying to impress her. He was acting like a big goofball in the arcade, winning her prizes and showing off his rifle skills in the old saloon, which of course he nailed just about every shot. He would have given the tickets to kids even if she wasn't there, but definitely basked in the appreciative glint.

A young girl with glasses and her brown hair pulled into a ponytail stood behind two older boys who were playing a video game. Although they had stacks of tickets, she had only a handful and tried to peer in. Were they her older brothers? They appeared to be in middle school and laughed and commented to each other as they played the game but ignored her.

Catherine walked over to the girl. "I have these tickets that I'm not going to use and I'm wondering if you'd like them?"

The girl's eyes widened. "Yes." She accepted with an eager nod and said, "Thanks." Her gaze drifted to the fluffy white bunny in Cate's other arm. "Wow, did you win that?"

"No, he did." Cate nodded toward Angelo.

"Wow," the girl repeated.

Cate turned over her shoulder. Somehow, she asked the question without saying the words. He nodded.

"I don't have a good place to put it." She handed the bunny to the little girl. "Would you be able to give it a good home?"

The girl nodded with eagerness. "Thank you." She hugged it to her chest. Then she trotted over to her brothers raising her hands to show her prize and all her tickets.

"Did you win all those?" one asked her.

The girl grinned and glanced back at Cate.

When she walked back to Angelo, he slung his arm over her shoulder. "You one-upped me with the bunny," he teased.

She shrugged and then smiled. "I couldn't help it. It made her so happy." She furrowed her brows. "Sorry I gave your gift away."

He laughed. "That's okay. I'll win something else for you another time."

A heavy weight of sadness passed through him, blocking his happiness. Since he was shipping out soon, if or when he'd have another opportunity wasn't a certainty. He lived in the moment with Cate, enjoying their limited time. He wasn't going to ruin it by brooding.

Back at the air hockey table, he raised the puck. "It's on."

She giggled. "That's some cutting smack talk."

He moved into position and grinned. "Don't need verbal sparring. I'll let my skills speak for themselves."

After losing three games, she conceded, "Fine, you kicked my ass. Are you good at everything?"

He shook his head. "Of course not."

"But, kind of. Football captain, Honor Roll, SEAL—and now, supreme air hockey challenger." With a sly grin, she added, "My competitive side isn't going to take this loss well."

"Can I soften the blow with a drink?"

She replied with an arched brow. "Yes, there's a pub nearby."

Twenty minutes later, they each had a cold ale in front of them as they sat at a high-top table in an Irish pub. Compared to the lively arcade, the dark-paneled bar was subdued. The din of conversation surrounded them.

"You keep staring at the pool tables," Angelo pointed out. "Do you want to play?"

"I do." She tilted her head. "Do you play?"

"Sure."

Both tables were occupied. He motioned to the dart board. "We can play darts instead."

"No, I'll wait."

When they'd nearly finished their beer, one of the couples left a table. Cate sprung over as soon as it was free.

"Damn. You really want to play this game."

She grinned and set up the balls in the triangle. "Want to break?"

He did. It didn't accomplish much other than spreading the balls across the table like a loud declaration that the game had begun. "You're up."

She nodded, keeping her eye on the table. After scrutinizing the position of the balls, she bent lower to take aim. The front of her shirt dropped down, offering him a nice view of her cleavage, which he lingered on. He dragged his gaze up. Catherine narrowed her aim with pinpoint precision as if firing through the sights of a rifle. No, that wouldn't fit her style. She was more into academics, especially science.

"You look as serious as if you're studying slides under a microscope," he joked.

"Angelo, please." Her voice was clipped.

"Please what?"

She didn't take her eyes from the ball. "Don't talk while I'm taking my shot."

She hit the white ball with such accuracy, she got two in pockets on opposite sides of the table.

"Nice."

"Thanks." On her next turn, she landed another one in. And then she sank two more and one again before it was his turn.

"Damn, girl."

She furrowed her brow. "I should have got the last one in. My calculation was a bit off."

Angelo took aim at the orange stripe ball and missed. Shit. This was not his game. He gritted his teeth. Could he at least get a couple in and not look incompetent in front of Cate?

It was her turn again. She struck each ball with precision fitting an elite sniper. The game ended soon after. She destroyed him.

"Guess you got your payback from the arcade," he teased.

"Did we never play pool before?" She replied in a sweet tone.

He laughed. "No. I think I would have remembered getting my ass handed to me that way."

"I couldn't let you win at everything, now could I?" She tilted her head and clucked her tongue. "That would be terrible for your healthy ego."

"Your competitive streak shines bright. I love it."

"With athletics, no. Academics, oh yes." She raised her eyebrows for emphasis.

"How does pool fit into academics?"

"It's all math and science. Geometry. Physics. It's all right there."

They finished their beers and walked back toward her neighborhood. He took her hand as they returned, enjoying the feel in his hand.

"I've got to admit, that turned me on to see you play like that. A natural pool shark."

She laughed. "That turned you on?"

"No, *you* turn me on. It's not just a physical attraction," he admitted. "It's talking with you. Your brain. I like spending time with you."

She gave him a brilliant smile. "Complimenting my brain. You sure know how to turn a neuroscientist on."

CHAPTER THIRTEEN

CATHERINE

After they left the pub, Catherine said, "Let's head down to the beach. I know that's where you want to spend time while you're back in Rhode Island."

Angelo raised a brow. "The beach at night. Sounds romantic. Are you trying to seduce me?"

She grinned. "Maybe."

They returned to her place to get her car, and she drove down to a small beach nearby. With darkness falling, it appeared quiet. Only a few couples walked it, one with a dog.

Catherine found a parking space without any trouble and grabbed a light blanket from her trunk in case they wanted to sit. He took it from her and tucked it under his arm. At the end of a walking path, she removed her sandals before stepping onto the sand.

"Good idea." He removed his sneakers and socks.

The moon cast a silvery glow over the sea. As they strolled the shore, cool sand slipped through her toes as they navigated around the seaweed and bits of broken shells. Angelo steered them to the water's edge.

He dropped his shoes on dry sand, the blanket with them, and then stepped into the water. Since he wore shorts, he didn't have to roll up his pantlegs. The water reached his ankles before he stopped and turned back to her.

He inhaled. "One of the things I miss the most is living near the ocean."

His appreciative expression was one she wanted to capture to memory. Romantic indeed. He looked so at ease out there with the sunlight dancing in ripples on the ocean around him. And gorgeous. Like a god come from the sea.

She followed his lead and breathed in the signature scent. The familiar sensory experience of the shore washed over her—its lulling sound of rolling waves and call of birds overhead. She tasted the salty tingle on her tongue.

"You're right. Since I grew up in Rhode Island, I suppose I take it for granted."

He nodded to her. "You coming in, Cate?"

With her sundress reaching just beyond her knees, she'd wade in without getting it wet. The brisk water on her feet shot a bolt of surprise over her that made her gasp. "It's cold!"

"It feels good."

As she acclimated to the temperature, the shock subsided. "Okay, it feels better now."

"Do you come to the beach often?"

"Not really. I'm not much of sunbather."

He took her hand. "It doesn't stop me from picturing you in a bikini. A tiny, string-tied one. Please say you have one of those."

She was far too uptight to wear a string bikini in public. "*That* might have to remain a picture in your imagination."

He swung their arms. "Oh hell no. I want to see you in the tiniest bikini barely held together by the narrowest of strings."

She lowered her chin and glanced up at him. "So, you wouldn't mind me wearing close to nothing in front of other guys?"

He groaned and gritted his teeth. "You're right. Only I get to see that view."

"Fine, if it's just you, I can handle it. Someplace private then."

He closed his eyes and smiled. After he reopened them, he added, "Out on a boat in the bay. Out where nobody can see if you decide to sunbathe on the boat in the nude."

She swatted his arm. "No way."

"Fine. You can leave it on. Are you free on Saturday? I'll see if I can borrow my Dad's boat for a few hours."

"Yes."

"Will you wear a teeny bikini for me?"

"Yellow polka-dot?" she teased.

"Sure, why not?"

She clucked her tongue. "Afraid I don't own one. I'll need to squeeze some time in to go shopping this weekend."

"Oh yes. I'm there."

Her mouth fell open. "What? I thought guys hated to go shopping."

"I'm not going clothes shopping. I'm going to watch you try on bikinis." He raised his chin and appraised her with a speculative glance. "Maybe some lingerie?"

She laughed. "You're packing a lot of outfits for me to wear in the short time you have left."

"Then you'll just have to send pictures to me."

She didn't know what to say, so she kept her mouth shut and gazed out to the horizon. This was the first time he mentioned anything about them having any sort of communication after he left Rhode Island. Maybe he just meant as friends—with string-bikini benefits.

Or could their time together lead to something more?

No. And she couldn't go there—even in her over-analytical brain.

"Where will you go from here?" she asked.

"Back to Virginia. And from there, who knows?"

She raised a brow. "If you did know, would you tell me?"

He laughed. "Depends."

"Part of being a SEAL, I guess."

"You guessed correctly."

While he stared at the ocean, she kept her questions to herself.

Once he turned back to her and they resumed walking, she asked, "Is there anything you can tell me about what you do?"

"What do you want to know?"

She shrugged. "It's something I remember you talking about. Being passionate about. Nothing anybody could say to convince you otherwise. So, is it all you thought it would be?"

Angelo gazed back out to the ocean, appearing to contemplate her question.

"It's been a tough year." His tone lowered as if weighed down with memories.

She stare at him, surprised he wasn't shutting down. Whatever it was had to be painful. "How?"

He released her hand and picked up a rock. After turning to the waves, he tossed it several dozen feet ahead. "I lost one of my teammates. A friend of mine." His voice turned low and gravely. "We were hit, and he took the brunt of it. I treated him, but it was too late. He'd lost too much blood."

Her chest seemed to rip out as her heart reached for him. "Oh, Angelo, I'm so sorry."

He exhaled, appearing to wrestle with something. "We've all lost someone. That was the toughest loss for me. Maybe because I felt so useless."

"You tried to help him." She yearned to comfort Angelo.

"Yeah. And although I know it's not my fault and you can't save everyone, I still wish I could have. It's just—difficult." He rubbed his hand over his beard.

"It sounds that way. Have you talked to someone about it?" She touched his shoulder, wishing he hadn't let go of her hand.

He gave her a sidelong glance. "You mean a shrink?"

"Something like that."

ANGELO

He grimaced and then nodded. "Yeah. We need to." He exhaled. "Multiple missions take a toll."

"If there's anything I can do, Angelo." She placed her hand on her heart. "I'm here."

He searched her eyes. "You're already doing more for me than you know." Then, he sucked in a breath and rolled his shoulders back. "I'm not trying to use this as an excuse—but on the night of the wedding when I asked you to dance, I had just been fighting off those images. I tried to refocus on something else." His gaze softened. "And then I saw you. A beautiful, bright vision to chase away all the darkness." He raised his hand as if about to touch her face, but then lowered it. "I admit—I might not have been completely with it yet."

She squeezed her eyes shut. What had she done—played that foolish game with him in retaliation. Shame burned through her. She reopened her eyes, afraid to look at him. "That awful way I reacted. I feel terrible."

"Hey, don't." He cupped her chin and searched her eyes. "I made you feel bad." He gave her a lopsided grin. "I've seen guys lash out a hell of a lot worse over a hell of a lot less."

She nodded in gratitude. "How often do you have images like that?"

"Not as much as I did after it happened. Please don't bring up PTSD. I know. We've all been screened for it. We've been educated on how to deal with it. I'm dealing with my issues, but it takes time."

"Okay."

"Being here helps give me a perspective from a distance." His gaze drifted back to the ocean. "Because lately I've been questioning things."

"Like what?"

For several seconds, the only sound was the rolling of waves. Would he not answer?

"How much longer I should do this." He faced her again.

"You mean being a SEAL?"

Angelo gulped. "Yes. It's all I ever wanted, but I've started to consider other options."

Catherine straightened. "In the Navy or out?"

"Either."

"With all your training and experience, you have so many options. In the medical field alone, you'd be such an asset."

"I've thought about that. My mom still works at a medical center. There's the Naval Health Clinic in Newport and so many hospitals in Boston." He took her hand again. "I like to help people. It's just—sometimes..." He swallowed. "You know?"

She gave him a sympathetic nod and squeezed his hand. "I know."

ANGELO

Why had Angelo revealed so much to Cate? He let out a giant exhale. Oddly enough, he felt lighter, as if he'd removed some of the density from the guilt and shame weighing him down. Had he unloaded too much onto her?

Time to lighten the mood.

"Enough of my problems." He gave her a mischievous smile. She was a stunning vision along the shore. The ocean breeze tossed her hair and he reached out to touch the soft strands. Then, he tucked it behind her ear. "Let's get back to talking about you and a bikini."

"Bikini?" she repeated, with a surprised expression.

"Or lingerie." He quirked his brows.

Her confusion evaporated from her expression, replaced by a warm smile that dazzled him. He could drown in those warm honey eyes. He caressed her cheek and she gazed up at him with expectation.

"When you look at me like that, it makes me want to do naughty things."

"Oh." Her voice rose with mock innocence. "What kind of things?"

He lifted her off the sand and she squealed, but then wrapped her legs around him.

"Dirty things." He lowered his head and kissed her.

After he put her down, they collected their things, and he led them under the pier. Once they were somewhat concealed beneath its shadows, he lay the blanket down and she scooted onto it. He slid his body over hers and covered her body with kisses.

He ran his hands all over her body, unable to touch her enough. Her dress offered him a glimpse of her skin, too tempting not to touch. Her soft shoulders. Her smooth calves. But now he had to explore what was hiding beneath the summery fabric. He reached beneath the hem and trailed his fingers up her thighs.

She grasped at him, pulling him tighter, and kissed him with more urgency. He cupped her sex and she moaned against his mouth, fueling his efforts. The scent of her arousal made him rock hard, agonizing for more.

He paused to glance at their surroundings. As the sky had darkened, the beach appeared to be void of people who might stumble upon them.

When he slid his fingers under the seam of her panties, she was wet. For him. He groaned with need. He slipped a finger in and she released a breathy sigh. Damn, he had to get rid of the panties fast to get more access.

When he tugged them over her hips, she gasped.

"Here?" Her eyes widened.

"Yeah. Why not?"

"I've never done something like this outside before." She scanned their surroundings. "Someone might see us."

"That's what makes it even hotter." He glanced around before he gave her another kiss. "Just roll with it. If you're uncomfortable, we'll stop."

A few seconds passed before the hesitant glimmer left her eyes. "Okay." She raised her hips.

He slid the panties over her legs and tossed them aside. "Doesn't the breeze feel good on your skin?"

She murmured, "Yes."

Without the barrier, he resumed his exploration, slipping two fingers inside her. She ran her fingers over the back of his neck, releasing soft moans against his mouth as he kissed her. When he rubbed his thumb over her nub, she shuddered, releasing the most beautiful sigh. Her breathy moans grew louder and more frequent with his quickening movements.

She was at the edge. He grew achingly hard as he brought her ever closer.

"I'm right there—" She exhaled in rough pants. "—I can't…"

He increased the pressure. "Yes, Cate," he encouraged.

She murmured something unintelligible and then gasped. As she bucked beneath him, he claimed her mouth and stifled the beautiful sounds that would alert anyone nearby. He throbbed with greater need, desperate to bury himself inside her.

Once her quakes subsided, he searched in his pocket to find the condom. Where the hell was it? Finally, he grasped it in victory.

"Do you want me, Cate?" he murmured.

"So much." Her voice sounded low and throaty.

"Are you ready for me."

"Yes." She reached for him.

He pulled back to push his shorts down and sheathed himself. As he slid the head of his shaft against her silky folds, primal need took over. He drove himself in, hungry to claim her. She was so wet, receptive to his touch, that he slid into her heated channel without restraint. She clutched him and moaned with pleasure.

As he lost himself in the sensation, an urge rose. He didn't want this thing between them to end.

"Fuck, Cate. You're killing me. I need you."

"You have me," she murmured, wrapping her limbs around him.

But for only a little longer.

CHAPTER FOURTEEN

CATHERINE

Sand rubbed against her body, both abrasive and soothing, but Catherine didn't care. This stolen moment under the pier—wild, passionate outdoor sex—was her hottest sexual experience yet.

She grasped Angelo's shoulder blades and wrapped her legs around his lower back. Her sundress rode up to her waist, exposing her to the cool night air.

Beyond the pier, the moon shone high. A kaleidoscope of stars shimmered in the darkening cloak over the ocean. Angelo wanted to spend time near the sea, but she never dreamed he meant like this. It was so naughty. So daring.

So unlike her.

He brought her out of her comfort zone, challenging her to try new things. Sex on the beach was simply a cocktail to her until now. Until Angelo came back into her life.

That tingling sensation stirred deep inside her once again, intensifying with a pressure that forced out all other thoughts. A sweet, decadent, desperate climb to the peak.

"Angelo, don't stop," she begged.

"No." He groaned. "Never."

It was a promise he couldn't keep, but that depressing thought was drowned by desire. Reaching for that precipice, she arched her body. He cupped her ass and drove in harder, pushing her to her limit. Each thrust made her gasp and hold on to him with more force.

Her body burned with a yearning she'd never felt before. Her skin was hot and tingly. Need rose within. A wild, blinding need that roared inside like an uncontrollable torrent.

She moaned. "I'm right there."

He drove into her harder, increasing the friction with each primal thrust. "Yes. Come for me, baby."

The dark sensuality in his tone touched a space deep within, untethering her last restraint.

She clung to him as her body trembled and she shattered. Spreading across the sky like the stars overhead. And then, floating in a blissful, mindless state. She clutched on to Angelo as if he was a lifeboat in the ocean.

"Fuck, Cate." His relentless thrusts grew more powerful. Feral.

He dug his fingers into her ass, and she yelped. His expression turned still and fierce. A low growl seemed to vibrate from his chest and rumble through hers. He throbbed inside her with his release while the rest of his body stilled.

For several seconds, neither of them moved. Their panting almost drowned the sound of the waves.

Dropping his damp forehead against her shoulder, he kissed her upper arm. She pulled him down onto her, relishing the touch of his muscular body covering hers. Their heartbeats pounded against each other in an almost symbiotic rhythm.

"Damn, girl, you're addictive." His breath warmed the side of her neck. "You're going to make it hard to leave next week."

Then don't. She clenched the words at her lips before they escaped. It would only make things more difficult for them both and wouldn't change anything.

THE NEXT MORNING, CATHERINE RUSHED THROUGH HER ROUTINE. Angelo had convinced her into a quickie, promising to cook breakfast while she got ready for work. She lathered herself with a coconut body wash, relishing the way Angelo had touched her minutes before.

The scent of coffee and pancakes greeted her as she descended the stairs.

He slid some blueberry pancakes on a plate for her and placed it on the dining room table. "For you, beautiful." He kissed the top of her head. Then he pulled out her favorite mug, an oversized one with the MIT logo, and poured coffee.

Her mouth watered. Bed and breakfast with Angelo were the ideal way to start her day. How was it Friday already?

"It smells delicious. Thanks, Angelo." She sat down and poured some Vermont maple syrup onto the pancakes. He sat across from her.

She took a bite. Sweet blueberries burst on her tongue mingling with the syrup. "Mmm." She smiled. "I could get used to this. Too bad you're only around until Wednesday."

Their eyes locked. She was teasing, but what passed between them was far more intense.

Had they only been together for less than a week? With all the time they'd spent together, it seemed much longer.

As if they were meant to be together.

She had to stop those thoughts before she set herself up for another heartache. Sure, this week she was on a high. But what happened next week after Angelo left? No other way to go except down. Was their time together worth it when it would inevitably crash?

Angelo gulped and speared his pancakes. "Yeah, well, Uncle Sam pays my check, so I go where they tell me." After he chewed a piece and swallowed, he put down his fork. "Can I convince you to take the day off and do something fun?" he asked with a suggestive wag of his brows.

He was masterful at changing the mood from intense to light, often with a sensual undertone. "Although it is a tempting offer, I can't." She frowned. "I took time off last week for the wedding."

"Okay." Angelo lifted his mug, her oversized black one that read Math Award in yellow letters. "Great size. I don't need to refill it ten times." He took a sip.

She'd kept it since middle school, unable to let it go. Now with it in Angelo's hand, she had a strange feeling of validation. Like he accepted her nerdy sentimentality—or maybe even appreciated it. He appeared so at home here, like he was a natural part of her life.

"Are we still on for sailing tomorrow afternoon?" she asked.

"Absolutely," he declared with a nod. "Is a teeny bikini going to be involved?"

"Oops." She winced. "I haven't bought one yet. I'll run to the mall tomorrow morning."

His eyes widened with an appreciative spark. "I get to watch you try them on, right?"

She'd just taken a sip of coffee and almost spit it out. "Oh no, no, no. Dressing room lighting is too harsh. I'll find something sexy, okay?"

"Deal." He toasted her coffee mug with his.

SATURDAY MORNING, CATHERINE RAN TO THE MALL TO FIND A bikini while Angelo prepared a lunch to bring out on the boat. A voice warned that she was getting too close to him. Soaring this close to the clouds could only end with a crash.

She tried to ignore it, instead pictured how the day might unfold. Would they make love on the boat? A small smile spread across her face and her skin tingled with anticipation.

When she reached her front door, the sound of Journey drifted out and the scent of something delicious wafted from her open window. Her place had previously lacked a liveliness without him there. As she opened the door, her heartbeat quickened.

He turned down the radio. "Hey, Cate." His grave expression didn't match his friendly greeting.

"What is it?" she asked.

He nodded to a pile of letters on her desk. "I brought the mail in and saw that one."

When she glanced at the white envelope on the top of the pile, her gut clenched. The meticulous tiny block letters were Trent's writing. The distinctive tiny capitalized letters were familiar from the previous letters. This time it was addressed to her *home*, and to Miss Catherine Boudreaux.

Her veins chilled as if injected with a liquid nitrogen. She raised her chin to offset her fear. "You went through my mail?"

"What the hell, Cate?" He looked at her as if her hair had turned bright orange.

Her hands turned clammy. "Did you open it?"

He flinched. "It wasn't sealed." He cocked his head and stared at her. "I was trying to be helpful."

"Helpful?" She repeated with widened eyes. "Did you read my mail?"

He glanced away. "It was open."

His reaction was confirmation that he had. Violation piled on top of violation. Trent's letter at her home address compounded by Angelo's invasion of privacy. Her ribs felt tight, lungs constricted.

"You can't do that, Angelo. That's so off limits." Her heart beat so loudly, drowning out the sound of the music. "These letters already bother me, but your reaction makes it worse."

"I'm not trying to freak you out." He turned his hands palms up. "I wanted to make sure he wasn't threatening you. I want to protect you."

"You don't have to protect me." She gritted her teeth and rubbed her forehead. "I'm not part of some SEAL mission."

"I know that."

She should stop. Anxiety pierced her tone as emotions whirled out of control. Trent's letters. Her confusion about Angelo. Her fears about what happened once he left—which was creeping up soon.

"Just because you're in my life for a week, doesn't mean you need to play this role." Her fears tumbled out in a maelstrom of anxiety she'd been suppressing. "What's the point when you'll be gone soon? Then what happens—I sit here alone, searching around my place all paranoid that someone is out to get me?"

"Cate?" He reached a hand out to her and then lowered it.

She strode into the living room and turned to face him. "What's going on between us is getting confusing." She motioned between them. "Too intense for a fling. And with all your SEAL wariness, it's messing me up. We're better off sticking to what we know this is."

He was right behind her. "And what is that?" He stared at her with furrowed brows.

"Sex." She raised her hand and avoided his gaze, instead staring at the weave in the taupe rug, one of the many locations in her place where they had made love. "Good sex for a few days before we each go back to our own lives."

When she glanced at him, his eyes flickered with pain. A blink later and it was gone, replaced by a neutral expression.

"Is that all you think it is?" His tone was low. Measured.

It's not what she wanted it to be, but she'd never admit how much this past week had affected her. Fantasies had spiraled into a longing for something more.

Impossible! He'd soon be off on another mission, leaving her behind. She was a fool. A dreamer. It would only exacerbate the hurt when he left.

The same as ten years ago.

No. She wouldn't let herself go through that anguish again, pining for someone like she had been for years.

"That's all it can be." She fought to keep a tremble from her voice. "You all but said it yourself from the beginning."

He didn't say a word, just stared at her with those intense eyes. She couldn't look at them.

Just sex, ha! Was she trying to kid herself? She couldn't even handle that. Her attempt at keeping things casual had already blown up in her mind. What a disaster. One that would leave her just as crushed—if not more so than in the past. She had to stay strong and protect herself.

"Maybe you should leave."

"Why?" His tone conveyed surprise.

Because it will be easier to get over you that way.

She took a deep breath and exhaled, crossing her arms over her chest. Not the time to waver. If she didn't protect herself from getting hurt again, she deserved the pain that she invited.

"This was probably a bad idea." She stepped away from him. "Yes, I think you should leave."

ANGELO

What the hell had just happened? Angelo's gut twisted as if an unseen enemy had rammed him with the butt of a rifle.

Sure, he shouldn't have read the letter, but the curiosity had driven him mad. It had been right there tormenting him. It was unsealed. He had to read it to gauge the threat. It was mostly confused ramblings from an incoherent mind and a messed-up drawing of what appeared to be a brain and hands.

Angelo stared at her, trying to read her body language. She'd adopted a defensive stance with crossed arms and raised chin. Although she stood as straight and hard as a statue there in her living room, a part of her appeared like she might crumble.

"Why do you want me to leave?"

"Because why bother when this only complicates things?" She brushed her hair out of her eyes with a frustrated wave. "You're leaving next week."

It was as if he'd been punched, beaten, and kicked while he lay on the ground trying to cover his internal organs.

Why was she pushing him away? Hadn't she been on board with them spending time together?

Maybe he'd never know. Who could understand women?

Ah, maybe it was the impending goodbye. He'd seen plenty of goodbyes turned ugly in the Navy. As a departure approached, someone could get drunk and lash out at their closest buddy. Lashing out was easier than saying goodbye. Especially when you weren't sure you'd ever see the person again.

He kept his tone gentle. "I'm here now, Cate."

"Exactly. Now. What happens when you're gone? It will be like ten years ago. You left, and I stayed here. P-pining for you."

That catch in her voice showed her vulnerability. All he wanted to do was take her in his arms. But that might be the worst thing considering she'd asked him to leave.

Instead he said, "I didn't know you felt that way."

She kept the defensive pose, but her eyes conveyed pain. Pure, raw, and brutal heartache. From him? How could he have caused her such anguish?

"It took a long time to get over you." Her tone softened. "Seeing you here again, I don't know if I ever truly did." She forced a smile and shrugged. "You're the one who got away."

His stomach twisted. "Cate." He hated hurting her. What could he say?

She sucked in a sharp breath and released it with an audible whoosh. "I'm not some young girl with a schoolgirl crush anymore. I won't make the same mistakes."

He swallowed a lump that formed in his throat, and it seemed to settle in his gut with a hollow thud. "Is that what you think this is—a mistake?"

She lifted her hands and dropped them. "What else can it be?"

He struggled with the answer, not sure himself. He ran his hands over the back of his neck. "Back then, we were so young and our relationship so new. It didn't make sense to try to make things work."

He'd seen many relationships unravel within months of enlisting.

"I know. Our lives veered into different directions."

He stared into her eyes, getting lost. Fuck, there was nobody like her. "But if you think that means I never cared about you, you're wrong."

She avoided his gaze and her bottom lip trembled.

They were ten years older now. More mature. With more life experience. Could they handle more of what the world threw at them if they faced it together?

The lump seemed to crawl back up into his throat. "What about now?"

Her eyes glistened as she shifted her gaze to the window. "What about now? Nothing has changed. You're still in the Navy, and I'm still here, now with a career."

It was a crazy idea, but he couldn't walk away from her without trying. Even if it meant she'd laugh in his face. He took a step closer to her. "What if we try to make it work?"

She stared at him with wide eyes. "Are you serious, Angelo?"

Right, he was an idiot. What the hell was wrong with him? She'd told them it was a mistake and he was about to propose a long-distance relationship. Why suggest something like that when it was bound to fail? And then he'd hurt her all over again.

"No, you're right." He stepped backwards. "Our lives are too different." After walking through the kitchen, he grabbed the doorknob and turned. "I'll leave you alone." He stepped outside but held on to the knob. "Do one thing for me, okay?"

The conflicted expression on her face gave him a glimpse of hope. Did she have any regrets about asking him to leave? She straightened. "What is it?"

"Have a friend or a relative stay here. Or at least have a neighbor check on you."

"Angelo..."

"It was wrong to go through your mail. I was worried about you, and I still am."

She exhaled. "I appreciate the concern, but I can't live my life in fear."

When he caught her eye, an overwhelming sense of loss hit him. With anguish in her gaze, she appeared to be just as devastated.

"Will you do one more thing for me, Cate?"

"What?"

His heartbeat amplified. "Give me a kiss goodbye?"

It felt like years passed as the silence engulfed him. She swallowed and then nodded. He released the doorknob and strode over to her. What was she thinking? He tried to read her thoughts in her glistening eyes. Was there any hope for them?

No, just pain—which he'd inadvertently caused. What a shit he was. He couldn't cause her any more.

Cate parted her lips. He cupped her face with both hands and slowly lowered his mouth to hers. When their lips touched, vibrancy bolted through him. She melted against him in the way he loved, clinging to him. With all that passion in her response, it couldn't be over, could it?

Don't read anything more into it. It's one last kiss goodbye.

He pulled his lips from hers with great reluctance. "Take care of yourself, Cate."

"Goodbye, Angelo." Her voice softened as low as a whisper.

As he walked to her front door on slow, heavy feet, he listened for her voice. Hoping she'd say "wait." Call him back.

She didn't.

He closed his eyes and took a mournful breath. It was over. After he reopened them, he pulled her key out of his pocket and placed it on her counter. He walked out of her place and closed the door behind him.

CHAPTER FIFTEEN

CATHERINE

Catherine attempted a difficult Sudoku puzzle on Monday morning to force Angelo from her mind. She'd dropped her head into her hands. Had she overreacted out of fear and made a huge mistake?

Her body still tingled from his touch. How would she ever forget the way he'd made her feel?

Raising her chin, she repeated her explanations to herself. It was better off this way. Their worlds were too different. It would have ended in a few days anyway. She saved herself more heartache.

And deprived herself of some tremendous orgasms.

She'd spent the rest of the weekend back to her typical, boring, pre-Angelo life. Sleeping alone was torment. Not only did she miss him, but she had Trent to worry about. It was hard to understand the severity of the threat. Angelo was over cautious, the university under. Where it lay was probably somewhere in between.

What she had to do was file a police report at work today. She looked at the latest damn letter from Trent. In addition to a letter was a drawing. It looked like a brain with hands all around it.

She headed to the university, hoping it would absorb her. She checked her email and jotted down a few top priority tasks on her to do list. Although she worked with technology, crossing things off paper held a certain amount of satisfaction. Somehow, it made her feel more productive, even on days with multiple interruptions. She wouldn't leave the office until she'd crossed off three things—even if she had to add a minor task first so she could cross it off. Yes, she was deluding herself, but it was a routine, and she liked structure.

Time to face the inevitable.

She entered the security office and stepped up to Frank's desk. "This letter was sent to my house."

Frank took the letter and read it. He glanced at the drawing and grimaced. With a grunt, he folded up the papers and returned it to the envelope. "I'll forward it on."

That wasn't good enough for her. Not this time. "Has anyone else reported such personal correspondence?"

Frank picked up a pen and clicked to open and closed three times. That was a nervous habit she hated. But it was the least of her concerns at the moment. "No. Just you."

"Shit." She didn't swear at work, ever. It wasn't professional. With her being the only one reporting the issue, the situation evolved from a nuisance to a far more disturbing one.

He leaned back and assessed her with a sharp gaze. "Are you all right, Catherine?"

"How can I be?" Her voice came out at a higher pitch, and she struggled to keep it level. She couldn't come across as being hysterical. After taking a deep breath, she exhaled and continued in a slower, rational tone, as if presenting the results of a study at a conference. Facts were rational. They would stop her from floundering.

"This man seems to have escalated his approach with me in particular. I thought Security was going to get involved, but I haven't seen any indication of that." So much that she didn't want to go home alone.

And if she wasn't so defensive Saturday, Angelo would've been there with her tonight. Who better to protect her than a Navy fucking SEAL?

Frank nodded. "Let me make some more calls."

That wasn't enough. Not anymore. "And I'm also going to be proactive. I'll talk to the police in my town." Since Trent had sent a letter to her house, she wanted the police in her jurisdiction to know what was going on.

"I'll make a note of it." Frank clicked his pen three more times.

When she returned to her office, she saw the package. Her pulse quickened.

Why? It was only small box no larger than a jewelry box left outside the door. It could be office supplies or something innocuous.

Then, why did her skin crawl as if suddenly infected with scabies?

With shaky hands, she entered her office. It took a solid two minutes of debate before she braved opening the package.

And then regretted it.

Inside was a mouse's head and a note with the familiar tiny handwriting.

Here's another brain you can destroy.

Half an hour later, two university officers sat on the visitor chairs in her office, taking notes. It seemed they asked her the same question in various ways.

When did this start?

How often?

Do you feel threatened?

Do you have any idea who it might be?

Do you have any ex-boyfriends who might have an issue with you?

Anyone else you think might have a problem with you?

They said they'd coordinate with the police in her area. After they left her office, she sagged in her desk chair. She had two more things she wanted to cross off her to do list but had zero motivation to do so.

Damn this guy for interfering in her life like this. Interfering with her work. He needed mental help and the sooner the better, so they could each move on with their lives.

Two more cups of coffee helped her push through to the end of the day. On the upside, the conversations kept her from thinking about Angelo.

As she drove home, she tried to convince herself she did the right thing. Not just for her, but for him.

After all, he had zero interest in having a relationship with her. With anyone. He'd made that clear. Her rule for hooking up with him meant not getting attached. It was supposed to be sex, pure and simple, to ditch ten years of regret. To forget about what ifs. To not pine for someone she couldn't have.

She stopped at a red light. A family of four walked by in the crosswalk—two parents and two boys. With beach towels poking out of the bag on the dad's shoulder, they were probably returning from a day at the beach. A family on vacation.

That's what Angelo was on—a well-deserved vacation. If anybody needed a break, it was a SEAL.

But he chose to spend time with you. Doesn't that count for something?

Those questions wouldn't help. She had to let him move on with his life and she with hers. That way nobody would get hurt. Because if the past was any indication, that person would be her.

THAT EVENING, TWO LOCAL POLICE OFFICERS MET HER OUTSIDE her place.

"We're going to take a look inside, okay?"

"Yes, please." She unlocked the door and stepped aside so they could walk in.

Her kittens ran up to them. Strange new people were irresistible. They sniffed at them and rubbed against their legs, but the police had things to do and moved through the apartment swiftly. How different from when Angelo knelt and gave them all the cheek rubs they could handle. She pictured it and a smile spread on her face. She swallowed the regret in her throat.

When the officers finished their search, they said, "No sign of any attempted break-ins. We'll notify the night detail, so they check in on you."

"Thank you." She exhaled. At least the intrusion hadn't gotten any further than her mailbox.

A twinge of discomfort in her stomach made her question what she was doing. Perhaps she was being overcautious, but if the police offered their services, she sure wasn't going to turn it down.

ANGELO

Angelo greeted his mother and brothers in the dining room. The scent of his mother's homemade tomato sauce filled the room. "Smells delicious."

"One of your favorites—your father's chicken parmesan." His mother motioned with a wave. "Grab a plate and join us."

Once he retrieved one, he sat with them. "Where's dad?"

"He'll be right back. You can start with salad." His mother put a bottle of wine on the table.

"You're having dinner with us again, Doc?" Matty's eyebrows shot up. "Something's up."

"Yeah, what happened to your days with family, nights with Cate plan?" Vince added.

Family. Although he loved them, he didn't love how they stuck their noses in his business—especially now. "Plans change," Angelo replied. "That's why you need to be flexible."

Matty exchanged a look with Vince. "Nah, I bet there's something more to it than that. Did she smarten up and toss you out on your sorry ass?"

Angelo stiffened. That was pretty much it. He'd questioned he was losing the mental sharpness and his overreaction to the situation with Catherine had confirmed it. If he couldn't even function like a normal person in the civilian world, how could he keep his mental focus as part of his team?

"Shit," Vince said. "What did you do? Or say?"

"Language!" His mother raised the wooden fork she was using to mix more oil and vinegar to a salad. She then handed the bowl to Angelo.

"Sorry, Ma," Vince said with a sheepish smile.

"I didn't *do* anything." Angelo clenched the fork as he scooped some salad onto his plate. "We had our fun, and that's it."

Matty studied him. "You may be able to sell that story to most people. But we know you better that than."

Angelo groaned. His spine was straight, body stiff, and he forced himself to shake out some tension. "What's the point of getting involved with someone? I'm going to be leaving in two days."

Matty coughed and muttered, "Bullshit."

Damn family. They could read him too well. His father walked in from the front door and greeted them with a box of cannoli. Angelo might as well wait before he announced the news. Saying it once was enough. After his father washed up and joined them at the table, Angelo took a deep breath.

Angelo loaded his plate with the chicken and pasta, as if he could smother his feelings with the comfort food. He took a bite. The delicious flavors were marred by the bitter words on his tongue.

He swallowed. "It's over. And it's for the best."

"What did you do?" Vince persisted.

"Why do you assume it was me?" Angelo raised his eyes to Vince.

"Because I've been on the receiving end of your big brother pushiness for many years."

Shit. Was that it? Yes, he'd pushed her too hard about the situation, and then had invaded her privacy. Bad, intrusive fuckin' move.

He didn't blame her for ending it. He fucked up. Her declaration was like a blockade that separated them. Trying to make it move might be as difficult as trying to move an armored vehicle.

"You're saying I'm pushy?" Angelo addressed Vince.

"You can be—overbearing," Vince replied. "When you think you know what's best for people."

"Well, maybe that's because I do—" he stopped himself. Talk about being stubborn and overbearing. "I only wanted to help her."

Hell, he spent his life helping people. The eldest brother and a corpsman, that's what he did. But maybe she didn't want someone to take care of her that way. She was smart and independent and didn't need the temporary attention of a SEAL to interfere in her life.

"What happened?" His mother asked in a sympathetic tone.

Angelo gritted his teeth. His usual mode would be to shut down the conversation and shove his emotions inside into a little compartment where it wouldn't affect him. But those little compartments weren't as securely fastened lately. It was if somebody had shaken his internal file cabinet, knocking it off center, leaving drawers half open and files scattered about.

Perhaps he needed to clear things out of his head and start with a clean slate.

Angelo dropped his fork. "I pushed her too far, and she pushed back. And out of her life."

His family stopped eating and stared at Angelo with interest. Damn. Nothing would get a DeMarchis to stop eating unless it was something big.

"I don't understand how anyone in the military can make a relationship work. You're separated from each other for long periods of time." Angelo faced his parents. "How have you made it work for so many years?" He didn't dare bring up the rough patch when they had separated when he was twelve. It wasn't like that was something any of them would forget.

His parents exchanged a meaningful glance.

"For me, there was no doubt your mother was the one," his father said. "It took months of pursuing before she agreed to marry me." He laughed. "How many times did I have to propose before you said yes, Marissa?"

"Three. And a half." She gave him a warm smile and turned back to Angelo. "I wasn't ready to take on such a role. I loved your father but knew it wouldn't be easy to be in a marriage where he'd be out at sea for months at a time. I always thought family life would be like the one I grew up in. My father was home for dinner at six every night."

"What made you change your mind?"

His mother's smile turned wistful. "Your father was worth it. Even if our marriage wouldn't be what I'd grown up picturing. It was better for us to be together for short periods of time than to be apart permanently. When you find the right one for you, all those ideas of what you think you want in your life vanish. Your heart recognizes what you need."

His mother's words swam in his head. Did he have a clue about anything he wanted anymore? He'd always thought that being a SEAL was everything he could ever want, and it had been for many years. Doubts had crept in. Maybe it was repeated missions taking a toll, and he needed a break. But something had changed in him. It could be part of growing older. Thirty wasn't far around the bend, and he didn't have that youthful gung-ho attitude that still floated around Matty like an exuberant glow.

Angelo had sworn off relationships because of his career. But being around Cate again had made him question that attitude. He'd had many flings over the past decade, but in truth, there never was anyone like her. The way he could talk to her about anything and delve deep into a topic, drew him to her as much now as it had when they were in high school. He'd even confided some of his innermost secrets to her, opened the doors to some of his tightly locked compartments deep inside his mind. Talking to her had made him feel better about those things that bothered him.

Would it be so wrong to have a relationship with her? Even if they had limited time, they'd still have time together.

He suppressed a groan. Fat chance of that happening since she'd booted him out directly as if giving him shipping orders to a new duty station.

"Angelo?" his mother said.

He pulled his gaze up to meet hers. "Yes."

Her look was understanding. "If you don't like how things are, why don't you do something about it?"

"It's too late. I fu—I mean, I messed up." He fixed his gaze on the chicken parm, but remorse stifled his appetite.

His father's eyes twinkled. "If I'd listened to your mother the first time she turned me down, you wouldn't be here today."

Angelo took a sip of wine. "What did you mean about a half proposal?"

"The fourth time I started to propose, I bent down on one knee and pulled out the ring." His father gestured with a grin in his eyes. "I started to speak, but your mother cut me off."

"I already knew what he was going to say as I'd heard it three times already," his mother added with a wave. "So, I said, 'Yes, you crazy fool. Now shut up and kiss me.'"

His father laughed. "So I did."

Angelo watched them. They gave each other a warm look. After all those years, all the bickering, all the hard times, and all the struggles, they still loved each other. Despite all the obstacles, they made it work.

He couldn't give up on Catherine yet.

CHAPTER SIXTEEN

CATHERINE

Catherine woke on Tuesday morning engulfed with uncertainty and regret. She went down into her kitchen to make coffee. Usually, she'd trip over the kittens on the way in, as they were anxious to have their breakfast. Where were they?

If she ever attempted to sleep in an extra hour on the weekends, they'd make their displeasure known and would pounce on her. Aurora would sit on Catherine's prone body to communicate her demand—*Breakfast. Now, human.*

Yet, no four-legged creatures scampered about this morning, rubbing their furry little bodies against her leg and meowing for attention. It was already 7:45am.

"Aurora. Ruby," she called.

No signs of them. Maybe they'd somehow locked themselves in a room. It wouldn't be the first time they'd closed a door. She looked inside the bathroom and closets. No meowing.

She searched their usual resting spots in her house. The pink and gray cat beds in front of the sunniest window. The sofa. The cat tree in the office so they could watch her as she worked —yet, just as often, they'd jump on her computer chair, keyboard, or all over Catherine to play.

A tightness seized hold within her chest cavity. Where were they?

She took a deep breath to relax the tension before she checked with Maria next door. "The kittens are missing. Did they happen to come visit you?"

They weren't outdoor cats but had escaped more than once. Usually, they'd find a way to outnumber her by running for it together when she opened the door—often while her hands were full of shopping bags.

"I haven't seen them. Want me to help you look?"

Maria's company might help keep Catherine's imagination from descending to a dark place. "That would be great. Thanks."

Maria closed her door and walked with Catherine into the parking area out front.

"Aurora. Ruby."

They searched anywhere a cat might hide, behind bushes and under cars.

Nothing.

"Let's check the courtyard," Maria said.

They cut through Catherine's townhouse, where she grabbed a plastic container of treats. Shaking that container would never fail to make them run for a serving.

Catherine and Maria exited through the glass doors leading to the shared courtyard. That area was open space with bushes at the perimeter near the residences. They peered under bushes and behind lawn furniture. A few neighbors saw them searching and asked what was going on. After Catherine told them, she asked them to keep a lookout for the kittens.

"Now where?" Catherine asked. With every minute that passed, not getting any closer to finding Aurora or Ruby, her anxiety spiked.

"They might have made it out onto the main road," Maria suggested.

Catherine's heart sank. They'd never been that far from home, as far as she'd known. "I hope not. They don't have any street sense."

They spent the next half an hour or so combing the neighborhood and notifying any passersby of the missing cats. As the search yielded no results, an unsettling tingle started at the back of Catherine's neck and intensified. What if they were out there somewhere lost and frightened?

"I'll go back and make flyers." Catherine would tape them to every telephone pole in the area. She'd post photos of the cats in every local group.

She couldn't make Maria stay out all day searching for her cats. "Thanks for helping me look. I guess they found something more exciting to do today." Catherine forced a smile. "They'll probably be back later for food."

Maria nodded. "I'll tell the neighbors to keep a look out. I'm happy to help look some more or hang up signs? I know what it's like. When my fur babies went missing, I was frantic."

Exactly. Catherine's ribs squeezed and every nerve seemed frayed. She forced herself not to panic. Sure, she was friendly with Maria, but that didn't mean Catherine would allow herself to fall apart in front of her.

She entered her house and took an involuntary sharp breath. Something wasn't right. The pillows on the sofa were not where she arranged them. She had a particular way of putting things, everything was lined up just so. She liked order. Everything had its proper place. She would never have left the pillows off center like that. And if the cats had moved them, they would've knocked them over, right? The contents on her desk were also askew. Pens not lined up in parallel made her skin itch.

Had someone been in there? Catherine exhaled and let out a shaky laugh.

Angelo. He had a key, remember?

No. He'd placed it on the counter before he'd left.

Maybe he'd found another way in. He was a SEAL, after all.

But that didn't make sense. Why would he enter her house, move stuff about as if searching for something, and then leave? He wasn't a stalker. And he had too much pride to come back and grovel for another chance.

She glanced around for other signs of intrusion. Nothing. Maybe the kittens had in fact been responsible for some mischief before they'd escaped, and Catherine hadn't noticed it earlier.

Or someone *had* been in there.

Her gut churned. One person came to mind. The same guy who had been bothering her with more personal actions in recent weeks.

What if he took the cats?

One thing she'd learned about intuition was that people often sensed when something was wrong, although they couldn't explain why. A mother would know something wasn't right with her child. A soldier would sense impending danger in battle. A police officer would sense something bad before responding to a call for a domestic dispute. The brain was fascinating, and she'd devoted her studies and her life to uncovering some of its mysteries. So, she wasn't going to ignore the warning.

She brought her phone into the courtyard, just in case an intruder was still inside. She glanced back at the brick townhouse. No, that didn't make any sense. If he took the kittens, he wouldn't stick around.

That was an *if.*

Catherine stood still as a statue. What should she do? Call the cops?

She grunted. They were there last night and had found nothing amiss. She could hear the conversation play out with the police.

"My cats are missing."

"Cats often hide. Did you look for them in closets, basements, that sort of thing?"

"Yes."

"They might have gotten outside. Have you checked with neighbors?"

"Yes."

"They may come back in a day or two."

"But with the recent letters and package..." How was she tying that to her kittens missing, which they'd probably chalk up to a case of curious cats?

She groaned at how ridiculous she sounded. Who would take her seriously if she said, "My pillows and my pens aren't lined up the way I like them—and my kittens are missing. Stop all the real work you're doing and help me find them!"

Was she being irrational? She couldn't find her kittens and her mind leapt to a farfetched conclusion. The idea of appearing foolish in front of anyone, even if they were strangers, repelled her and made her muscles taut. She'd rather search for the cats herself, even if it took her all day and night.

If the cats didn't return by the time the police stopped by later that day, she'd mention how they were missing and her suspicions that someone had been in her place. She'd present it with rational facts, not hunches.

In the meantime, Catherine would keep searching for the cats. She couldn't go to work without knowing they were okay. After texting her boss to let him know she'd be in later, she trekked again through the courtyard, keeping watch for Aurora and Ruby slinking out from under any bushes. A yearning grew to reach out to someone. Someone who had been looking out for her, yet she had turned him away. Someone she would have spent the day with, sailing on the bay, instead of being alone and swallowed the bitter taste of regret.

She raised the phone with a shaky hand. Damn it. She'd felt so safe around him, and her world was now so unsteady. She took deep breaths and counted to seven before he answered.

"Angelo, it's me, Catherine."

One. Two. Two seconds went by. Two long seconds of ear-piercing silence. Had she made a mistake by calling him? Would he tell her he had enough of her crap and to leave him alone?

"Hey, Cate. How are you doing?" His voice sounded neutral, not revealing anything.

"Fine. Sorry to bother you, but are you busy right now?" She couldn't tear him from something important, like family time, for something that might make her seem neurotic.

"Just watching soccer with my dad. Why, what's up?"

"Oh." She clutched the phone more tightly and paced. "I don't want to interrupt."

"You're not. I'm barely paying attention. I'm surprised to hear from you after—well, you know."

His voice comforted her. Something about him made her feel safe and—appreciated. Maybe even cherished. She'd been a fool to push him away. And for what? Her independence or something like that? She wasn't even sure. All she knew was she wanted him here with her now. She *needed* him.

"I know, and I'm so sorry about that. I overreacted and I've regretted it ever since."

"Cate, are you all right?"

His concerned tone soothed her frayed edges. She took a deep breath lest she expound all her fears in one rambling, incoherent sentence. "This might sound strange," she began. "But my cats are missing." Good, she kept her voice level despite her shakiness. "I've looked for them everywhere. I know it sounds crazy, but I think someone might have been in my place." Her voice had a higher pitch on those last words. So much for keeping her voice steady. She pursed her lips before she added anything else that would make her sound hysterical.

After hearing Angelo's voice and revealing her fears, they eased. Maybe she was freaking out over nothing and there was a perfectly reasonable explanation. The kittens might have knocked things askew and then found a way to sneak out. Worry had scrambled her ability to think straight, jumping to the worst conclusions.

"Have you called the police?" Angelo asked.

"No. They were here last night and will check back in today, so I figured I'd tell them then. Yesterday, I received a disturbing package at work and talked to them." Her trembling voice cracked. "I was wondering—I'm hoping—could you please come over here?"

He didn't say anything for two seconds. "I'll be right there, Cate."

Catherine hung up the phone, and then did another round searching through the parking lot. She returned to her place. A white envelope peeked out from under her kitchen door. Oh good! Maybe one of the neighbors had found the kittens and left a note.

She covered her heart and rushed over. When she attempted to pull the corner, it was jammed too tightly. She opened the door and stepped inside. Then she picked up the envelope and closed the door.

It was her name in *his* handwriting.

Shit. Her hands turned clammy and her heart pounded in her chest.

Should she open it, or wait for Angelo? She guessed she wouldn't be happy reading the contents of that letter.

She paced through her living room, counting her steps, and sneaking glances at the out-of-place envelope, a sign that something wasn't right in her otherwise orderly space. Her mind raced, envisioning countless possibilities for what was written inside.

Curiosity for their well-being won out. If it mentioned something about them, she had to know. She strode over to the envelope, picked it up, and pulled out the letter with trembling fingers.

If you call the police, you'll never see them again.

At least not alive.

Catherine dropped the letter as if it were on fire. She almost lost control of her bladder. He'd taken her kittens and threatened to kill them. Her innocent, defenseless kittens. What kind of person did that?

One kind, in particular. A person who could hurt animals was more likely to hurt people.

She covered her mouth and backed away from the letter. What could she do?

Oh, the poor kittens. She crossed her arms across her chest. She pictured their adorable faces with inquisitive eyes. Those two playful, lovable maniacs. What would he do to them if she called the police? Graphic images with blood and knives and water and suffocation tormented her. She forced them away. She wouldn't let the fear incapacitate her. She had to think clearly. Taking the wrong action to enrage an already unhinged man was dangerous.

What to do next? She paced through her living room. Angelo was coming. Thank God. He was used to making decisions at critical times. She'd show him the letter. They'd figure something out together.

While she sorted out that plan, she ran upstairs to use the bathroom. After searching for the cats that morning, her bladder was ready to burst.

As she washed her hands, she glanced at herself in the bathroom mirror. Her face was pale and eyes tired beneath her glasses. Her hair wasn't even brushed. Ugh. She looked like she felt. A wreck.

Catherine entered her room and put on a clean light blue T-shirt over her black yoga pants. She ran a brush through her hair with more vigor than necessary.

"Why have you ignored me?" a man spoke.

Fear clogged her throat. The unexpected and unfamiliar voice shot spiders skittering over her skin.

She spun around and faced a stranger. A tall, lanky man who appeared to be in his mid-twenties stepped across the threshold. Into her *safe* space. He had trimmed brown hair and a clean-shaven face and wore jeans and a button-down gray shirt. Like many men on campus. Not how she pictured him. Although she didn't have a concrete image in her mind, the confused content of his letters led her to believe he'd appear more disheveled.

"You must be Trent." She raised her chin to project defiance rather than the fear crawling inside. "Why are you here? And how did you get in?"

"A pleasure to meet you at last." He bent forward in a mock bow.

"What have you done with my cats?" Her voice trembled, but she kept her head high. She wouldn't give him the satisfaction of her cowering.

His eyes flickered with an alarming glimmer. "I needed to get your attention. And it worked." He let out a hearty laugh, but then glared at her. "I've warned you to drop the project, but you ignored me."

He narrowed his gaze. The eyes of someone dangerous.

"Worse, you got the cops involved." He took another step. "So, I had to take a more drastic approach."

She stepped back. His demeanor darkened as he walked in, narrowing the distance between them like a predator closing in on prey.

No way. She clutched the hairbrush more tightly. Fighting with it wasn't the best option, especially against a man who loomed over her with a face full of menace.

But what alternative did she have? If she tried to run, she'd have to slip past him *and* run down the stairs *and* outside, hoping he wouldn't catch her.

Then again, she might not even get by him in the confined space.

"I don't like what you've been doing." He took another step toward her, breaching deeper into her bedroom. An odd scent rose from his clothing. Cloves. He must have smoked clove cigarettes.

"Stay away from me." She moved back and raised the brush.

"You shouldn't have ignored me. Don't you think I know what I'm talking about?" His expression contorted with pain. "I've been suffering from what the government has done to me." He tapped his temple. "In here. My life has been a twisted, endless hell because of people like you."

"I haven't done anything to you." She backed to the window. It was now closed, which he must have done. With him approaching, escaping was the better option, but how? Every muscle screamed *run*.

"Where are you going?" His voice turned as sugary as soda. "I just want to talk. That's it. Talk."

With his threatening demeanor replaced with a friendly smile, he almost appeared genuine. Like a politician trying to sell a lie.

"Talk?" Maybe she could buy enough time to get to the door by keeping him talking. She backed along the wall inching toward the door, bumping into a framed photo on the wall. It wobbled but didn't crash to the ground. She navigated around it. "About what? About why you're fixating on me, a stranger who has nothing to do with you."

"Ah, but you do." He raised his index finger and pointed. "It's people like you who screw up people like me."

"You're wrong." She shook her head in defiance. "My research on memory is to help people, not harm them."

He snorted. "You see what you want to see. Believe what you want to believe. It doesn't change the consequences."

What kind of consequences? Her breath rate escalated. Her room never seemed so small and claustrophobic. This man was dangerous.

She backed away. He strode faster.

"Stay away from me." She sprinted to the doorway.

As soon as she passed the threshold, he grabbed her arm and yanked her back.

"Let go! Let go!" She punched and kicked at his mass and squirmed to escape.

He tightened his hold.

"Help! Help!" she screamed.

Shit. Would anyone hear her? Fucking insulation. That soundproofing feature that had appealed to her when she was looking for a place now threatened to swallow her in a silent tomb.

Trent threw her on her bed. "Quiet!"

He slapped her. The sharpness resounded and she cupped her cheek, now hot. The urge to escape swelled. She jumped off the bed and darted to the doorway again. He clutched around her waist and flung her back onto the bed. He straddled her and grabbed a pillow, forcing it onto her face. She gasped, fighting for air, and she struggled to squirm out from under his mass.

"I told you I want to talk, but you refuse. Making it more difficult for both of us. If you shout out one more time or try to run, I will suffocate you. It's too easy. Just like this." He pressed on her head.

The instant blackness was followed by a lack of oxygen. She pushed the pillow up. No use. Terror radiated from her spine. She was going to die here. Like this.

No. No. No.

She clawed at his arms, his hands, anything.

He yanked the pillow away. "Bitch. You drew blood."

She gulped for air. Never had she appreciated oxygen so much.

Breathe, breathe, breathe.

Trent pinned her by the forearms with such force, she cried out.

"Quiet," he reminded her. He bent close to her ear. "I don't care how much it hurts. You try to draw any attention, you die. Consequences, remember?"

"Okay." She squeezed back scalding tears.

He pulled her off the bed and pushed her into the antique rocking chair. Then he sat down on her lap with his back toward her, crushing her. Something rough wrapped around her wrist. No! He was tying her to the chair. A family heirloom became a prop in her prison. He continued with her ankles. She wiggled and kicked. It didn't prevent him from tying her ankles to the chair, but they weren't as tight as her wrists and she had at least some movement.

She struggled to slip out. More punches. More kicks. It was futile. His weight crushed down on her, preventing movement.

No matter how hard she fought Trent, he overpowered her. One wrist restrained. Then the other.

She bucked, desperate to escape her restraints. Flight didn't work. Neither did fight. "Why are you doing this to me!"

He cocked his head. "Because you're one of them."

"One of who?"

He paced before her and tapped his head. "You're leading a project on memory. For the *government*. I've read about you. And then I tried to warn you what you're doing, but you wouldn't listen."

"It's to help people. The more we know, the better we can help with conditions like Alzheimer's and—"

"No. That's what you tell yourself. They'll use it to control people. They already have with me!" His expression turned feral and unfixed and his gait evolved into a prowl. "They put something in my brain. And I haven't been able to remember things right ever since then."

She took long, deep breaths. He was tormented by what sounded like delusions, which might be helped by therapy or medication. If he hadn't broken in and tied her up, she might have felt more sympathy.

In a calm voice, she said, "I am not someone who you think has harmed you."

He scowled. "No!" Spittle dropped from his lips. He clutched his head. "Don't try to tell me I need help. No more experiments."

What experiments? Was any of what he said real, or all a delusion?

He faced her again with a leer. "I know you called him, and he's on the way. Don't worry, I'm prepared."

Dread hit her like a head-on collision.

"The police will be here any minute," Catherine cried. Minute was a stretch. They'd check on her at some point—probably when it was too late.

He laughed. The glimmer of excitement in his eyes shot a fresh quake of tremors throughout her flesh.

He pulled out a knife and admired it. "Let them come."

CHAPTER SEVENTEEN

ANGELO

*A*ngelo returned to the deck where he'd been relaxing with a beer and watching a soccer match with his father under the morning sunlight.

"Can I borrow your car?" Angelo struggled to keep his tone steady. The anxiety in Cate's tone set him on edge.

His father glanced up. "You missed Italy score."

The game could wait. "Dad, did you hear me?"

"Your brothers took it to the tackle shop." This time his father kept his eyes on the TV.

Angelo groaned. "Did Ma take her car?" She'd said she was getting a few things from the farmer's market.

"No. She walked."

"I need her car." Urgency rang through his voice.

"Why so tense?" His father studied Angelo.

"Cate asked me to come by."

"Oh," his father responded in a knowing tone, as if suddenly understanding it was girl problems. "Check the basket for her keys or the spare set."

Angelo ran inside and fumbled with the collection of keys in the seashell-accented basket his mother kept by the front door. Why the hell did his parents need so many keys? They had one house and two cars. With the countless sets of keys on key chains from various states they'd visited, it was more like they were renting out rooms in a damn B&B.

Angelo fished through them, along with a collection of junk mail that would never be acknowledged and magazines that would never be read. The urge to rush to Cate intensified.

Finally, he found the right one to his mother's Fiat. It was fastened to a Maine — Vacationland key chain with an image of a lobster. He shouted to his father through the screen door.

"Found it."

His father opened the screen door and met Angelo in the hall. "Your mother is going to ask me two things when she gets back. One—when are you coming back with her car? And two—are you going to be back for dinner? We were thinking of going out tonight."

"I don't know. I'll call as soon as I can."

His father cocked his head. "Don't screw it up this time."

Angelo gave him a lopsided smile. "Thanks for the sound advice."

He rushed out the front door and into the driveway. Once seated in the tiny Fiat, he backed out of the driveway in such a hurry, he didn't see Matty driving up towards him in their father's car.

"Hey, oh!" Matty beeped and stuck his head out the window. "Where did you learn to drive, Doc? Med school?"

Angelo ignored him. He didn't have time for the banter. He waved and drove off.

Cate had called him. She was upset and had reached out to *him*. He damn well wasn't going to let her down.

Angelo gunned it down the tree-lined road and onto the main street quicker than necessary. His stomach churned. He pounded on the steering wheel. "Fuck."

The letters messed with his head and led him to screw up his chance with Cate. But he couldn't turn off the radar. He was too fucked up by years of bullshit and missions turning FUBAR, followed by despair. It always took its toll.

What was in the package she received? Who the hell was this fucker and why wouldn't he leave Cate alone?

He followed the signs to head north to Providence, seeking out glimpses of nature. Woodland with its secret wildlife, water with sunlight reflecting on the surface—those peaceful settings calmed him.

Maybe he was fucked up, but he could learn to relax around certain people. Like his team and his family. And Cate. The encounter with the little girl and the bunny in the arcade came to mind. She had always been kind.

Memories returned as he drove from one mile into the next. When they'd been finishing out their senior year, and he'd told her of his plans to enlist in the Navy, she'd been surprised.

"What about college? With your grades and scores, you could get into a top school."

"It's not part of my plan, Cate. I'm going to enlist, and I want to be one of their best. My goal is to be a SEAL."

"A SEAL?" She'd raised her brows. "You do know how difficult that is?"

He'd laughed. "I do. It's a long, tough road ahead."

She'd given him a forlorn look. Their futures were headed in two different directions.

How had they grown so close again so quickly only to have it detonate like a grenade—with little warning, resulting in sudden devastation?

Angelo gripped the steering wheel more tightly, but then let off the gas when he spotted the speed limit, and he'd gone twenty miles over it. Damn it, why had this nut job fixated on her and her work? Countless contractors worked on projects, yet this guy had to pick Cate. *His* Cate.

Not technically, but didn't he have some sort of claim to her? Not really. Nothing beyond a short-term fling on leave and even that had fizzled.

That wasn't what he wanted. He wanted more from her. A relationship. A promise to be there for each other. If she'd have him.

Angelo struggled to stay close to the speed limit as he drove and avoided weaving in and out of traffic. After taking more deep breaths, he loosened his death grip on the wheel.

He fixed his gaze ahead. The minutes dragged until he finally left the highway and drove on the main street that led to her neighborhood. As he passed the pub where she'd kicked his ass in pool and the arcade where he'd won a stuffed bunny for her, memories flooded him. Happy ones. Being around her brought him a contentedness he hadn't felt since—he couldn't exactly remember when.

And their time on the beach would be something he wouldn't forget soon. He'd never curse the sand again.

Finally, he turned onto her tree-lined road and spotted the brick townhouse complex where she lived. Warmth clashed with regret. He should have been there already, woken up with her in his arms.

After he pulled up into an available spot in her parking lot, he broke into a near trot on the walkway.

He rang the bell. Ten impatient seconds ticked by. He knocked. "Cate?" He paused, waiting. "Cate, it's me."

Thirty slow seconds later and no answer. His heart pounded. What the hell? Why would she call him over and then not answer the door? Had she changed her mind about seeing him?

Or something worse. She couldn't answer the door.

He reached into his wallet for the key. Fuck. He'd left it on her counter when she'd ended it.

Likely for the better. His impatience would tempt him to use it. And if he barged in like he owned the place, she'd be pissed.

He rang the bell again twice more. "Cate, it's Angelo." Then he paced and forced himself to wait.

CATHERINE

Angelo came. Catherine's heart jumped in jubilation. The third time he rang the doorbell and called for her, dread settled in her gut with a repetitive thud.

Trent glowered at her and then smiled. "Time to break lover boy's heart." He paced before her with the knife.

She yearned to scream and warn Angelo.

Trent pointed the blade at her face. "Don't be stupid."

Angelo pounded on the door. "Cate."

Trent waved the knife toward the window. "Get rid of him."

She exhaled. Yes, getting Angelo away from them, to safety, was preferable than the dark scenarios she'd envisioned.

"Tell him you found the cats," Trent directed. "And you're busy."

She pursed her lips. "Okay." Maybe she could give him a signal at the door. Some sort of eye twitch or mouth *Call the Police*.

She struggled against the restraints. "Can you untie me so I can go tell him?"

He barked out with laughter. "I'm crazy, not clueless." He raised his chin with a half-nod. "Tell him from here."

"He's not going to hear me."

"Don't say anything besides what I told you to say." He pointed the knife at her for emphasis.

She recoiled but recovered. "You don't have to remind me you have a knife," she snapped. "I get it."

Trent glared at her before he cracked the window.

"Cate." Angelo knocked louder. "It's Angelo. You told me to come over."

She took a shallow breath and sighed. "Sorry, Angelo. I can't come to the door right now."

Did her voice sound off? Yes, of course. How could it not? A guy had tied her up and threatened her with a knife. Would Angelo catch it?

"What about the cats?"

"Um—" She glanced at Trent, who narrowed his eyes at her. "They're fine. I found them."

"What?" Angelo paused. "Why didn't you call me back then?"

His voice was clipped. From confusion or exacerbation?

"I'm so sorry, Angelo, but—*I'm tied up right now.*"

Trent hissed and moved the knife to her throat. "Easy," he whispered. "Tell him you'll call him tomorrow."

"What the hell's going on, Cate? Why don't you let me in?" After a pause, he added, "It's not like we don't have things to talk about."

Her heart thumped in her chest cavity. An ache spread in her gut. Oh, how she wished she could do what he suggested. Not just talk to him but see him. Be with him.

Hot tears stung hear eyes and regret flooded her. What a fool she'd been to end it. She'd ruined what could have been the best week of her life.

"Tell him," Trent commanded.

She sucked in a shaky breath. "Angelo, this is a bad time. I'm sorry you came all this way. I'll talk to you later."

Although it killed her to send him away—the only one who could help her in this situation—at least she could keep him safe.

Her heart crashed into her ribs. He'd never know the real reason why she had to push him away.

ANGELO

Something was wrong. It didn't take a whole lot of brain cells to put that together.

The odd emphasis she put on the words when she said she was tied up was enough to trigger his suspicions, not to mention the vast difference in tone from her phone call and then pushing him away. Why had she changed her mind?

It could be a woman thing, he supposed. And who the hell could figure out that code but other women.

He gritted his teeth. No, it was more than that. Those words echoed in his head—*tied up.*

He walked to her kitchen window. The curtains were parted enough so he could peek in. He assessed the interior for any signs of something off. Furniture upturned. Some sign of struggle.

Nothing like that. He took a closer look, scanning the details as he'd been trained to do. Then he noticed it—something most people would overlook. Her pillows weren't lined up on the sofa like square soldiers. That wasn't like Cate. It didn't fit her compulsive neatness.

And then on the floor—a white letter.

Shit. Considering what had happened the last time he'd looked at her mail, maybe he should step back.

But still, he couldn't shake the feeling that Cate was in trouble.

On the off chance that it was unlocked, Angelo turned the doorknob. No such luck.

If he hadn't left the damn key to her place, he would've let himself in. Sure, he'd have to face her wrath, but at least he could ensure she was safe.

The kitchen window was cracked a few inches. If it wasn't locked, he could push it open. But hell, he'd never get his body through that small space. Maybe there was another open window. It was summer, and she preferred to leave windows open. He laughed, thinking of one of their discussions. Now, he agreed with her argument. Leave all the damn windows open—and unlocked.

He scanned up to her bedroom window again. It was now closed. Interesting.

Angelo might have been around danger for too long, but he couldn't ignore the signs. Perhaps he was being paranoid and acting as insane as the nutter who wrote her letters, but he'd have to take that risk. If she was in danger, the first suspect would be that creep. And if somebody was in there with her, he wanted him to think Angelo had left.

He let out a big exhale. "Okay, Cate. I get it. I'm leaving."

He moped down the walkway with his head hanging low, in case he was being watched. He cut into the parking lot and moved down the block. He scanned every part of the scene as he moved through parked cars, his instincts fully engaged. Movement in the back of a black sedan caught his eye. Cate's kittens stared out. When they saw him, they pawed the window and meowed for his attention.

This wasn't her car. Fuck. She'd lied about finding them, probably because she had to. Someone had to be coercing her to say those things. And he might be armed. And if it was that guy...

"Hold on, kitties. I'll be back."

He had to get to Cate first.

He ran back toward her place, seeking concealment en route. Hiding behind cars. Creeping along the shadows at the side of the building. He rushed through the gates into the courtyard. Nobody was lounging around, thank God. A window was open on the second floor where she had her office. It was a normal size window, not that tiny one in the kitchen, and he could fit through it.

Angelo scanned the exterior to see what he had to work with to climb up. A brick building with window ledges. He grunted. He'd scaled worse.

A drainpipe. Deeper recesses in between bricks where he could get a footing. Windowsills. A few vines. He assessed the optimal route to climb and then stuck his fingers in between bricks. Time to go for it.

Once he pulled himself up and supported his weight on a brick footing, he maneuvered up and over the bricks. His pulse quickened, but he ignored it and pushed on.

Reach, reposition, support, adjust.

Only once he'd supported himself on a window ledge, did he think of a complication. If one of the neighbors saw him, they'd call the police. Hell, maybe *he* should've called the police. He was so used to responding to emergencies that he didn't think of the other option until he was halfway up the wall. It wasn't as if he could call 911 for backup when on an overseas mission.

If there was nothing off inside her place, and she learned of him trying to break in, she'd never talk to him again. Shit, he couldn't leave yet, not until he knew she was safe.

Just a few more feet and he would make it to the open window. Sure, it was open, but the screen was there. He had to knock that out without making much noise.

He reached over to grasp a drainpipe for support. Then he took a deep breath and released his hold with one hand so he could apply pressure to the screen. He forced the metal on the edges inward. If he lost his grip or slipped, he was fucked.

So, don't do either of those things.

The metal bent. He pushed the screen in, careful not to use too much force. If it fell to the ground, it might as well set off an alert screeching, "Intruder!"

With that obstacle removed, he forced his way into her study. He rolled in, rose to his feet, and exhaled.

He was in.

CHAPTER EIGHTEEN

CATHERINE

Angelo was gone. A maelstrom of despair threatened to engulf her. She took deep breaths to control the sinking sensation. No sense of dwelling on his absence. She had to use her head. Trent still clutched the knife at his side.

"This isn't the way to make things better." Catherine struggled to keep her voice steady. "We can talk about a better option."

"No!" Trent spun in a semi-circle and faced her. "I told you, enough doctors."

He'd seen some, but what had happened? Was he supposed to be on meds? Were they involved in his perception about his memory issues?

Movement from the doorway caught her attention. Angelo burst through. She gasped.

Before she could speak, he hurled something at the side of Trent's head. The object crashed to the floor. Trent howled as he leaned forward.

"Angelo!" she cried.

He didn't reply. With a determined expression, he moved a pair of scissors from his left hand to right, thrusting it like a weapon. He lunged at Trent and wrestled him to the ground. Within a few, pulse-racing seconds, Angelo had disarmed him.

He threw the knife across the floor near her feet. She reached for it, but the damn rope didn't allow any leeway.

Trent struggled against Angelo. "Get off me!"

Angelo wrestled Trent onto his stomach and pinned his arms behind his back. "Shut the fuck up."

She searched for something to help Angelo. The black and silver object he'd thrown at Trent was her stapler. Her chest heaved. How resourceful. Angelo must have figured out something was wrong, broken in, and grabbed whatever he could use as a weapon.

"The rope." She attempted to point, but the restraints held her in place. "Next to the bed."

Angelo caught her gaze. Time slowed and her heartbeat echoed in her ears. He came for her. He wrestled an armed intruder to rescue her. He could get hurt. Killed. In that moment, it all rang clear. She'd pined for him for ten years for a reason. He was the one. Obstacles didn't matter and time and distance wouldn't change her feelings.

That had to wait. She motioned with her chin. He followed her gaze and reached for the rope. It was out of reach.

Damn it, he couldn't grab it without him relinquishing his hold on Trent.

Angelo moved back, releasing some of the pressure on Trent, who used the opportunity to try to break free.

"Don't fuckin' move," Angelo said, smashing Trent's body back to the floor.

"Wait. Let me try." The rope on her ankles allowed enough leeway for her to move a few inches. She hobbled over on the chair, scraping across the wood floor. Scooting barely an inch after frustrating inch. Her body heated under this odd exertion. It would take a hell of a long time at this rate.

"I got him, Cate," Angelo said. "He's not going anywhere."

"Fuck you!" Trent struggled against Angelo straddling him.

"Didn't I tell you to shut the fuck up?" Angelo twisted Trent's arm back, making him cry out. "You're lucky I don't do worse. Don't ever mess with my girl."

My girl. Those words sent a ripple of delight through her despite the seriousness of the situation. She continued her awkward hobble.

After what seemed like hours, she reached the rope. Now the next part of the challenge—getting it over to Angelo. If she kicked, the rope could go in any direction, even farther from where she wanted to go. Especially since her restraints didn't allow much movement.

Think of it as a pool table. Where do you want the ball to go?

Sure, her foot and a ball of rope wasn't the same concept as a pool stick and a billiard ball, but it all came down to geometry and physics.

She maneuvered with clunky movements to turn to a more optimal position. Then she outlined her strategy. One. Two. Three. She kicked the rope.

Without much momentum from the restraints, it didn't land as close as she'd hoped, but it was in arm's reach. Angelo reached back along his hip and grabbed the rope. While keeping his weight pinned on Trent, he tied him face down to the thick bed post legs.

Angelo then rushed to her and worked on the knot fastening her wrists. After he freed them, she pulled them apart, ready to throw her arms around him. He moved on to her legs and removed the tightness binding her ankles. Although the rope burns stung her skin, relief flowed through her.

She leaped out of the chair and into his arms. "Oh, Angelo."

"I got you, Cate."

He pulled her into such a tight embrace, it was like being restrained again, but in a far more enticing hold.

He pulled back just enough to search her eyes. "Are you okay?"

"Yes. Now that you're here. I regret everything. I was a fool."

"No, I pushed you and I deserved it. I'm sorry."

"Oh, Angelo."

He covered her face with kisses and then cupped her cheeks in his hands. Her heart pumped wildly, as if burning from the intense happiness rushing through her. All she wanted to do was touch him and kiss him and reassure herself that they were together and safe, but now they had to deal with Trent, who was threatening them through strings of curses.

. . .

Moments later, police swarmed her place. Had someone heard the struggle and called 911? Time passed by like a whirlwind as they arrested Trent and seized the knife. Investigators spoke to her and Angelo and took their statements.

"I think I know which car is his," Angelo told an officer and then went to show her.

While Catherine waited for him to return, she tried to process what had happened. He had scaled the building to reach her. She flushed. If he hadn't come for her…

No, she wouldn't go down that dark path. Not now.

Angelo returned a few minutes later, holding two squirmy kittens in his arms. Bending down, he released them. "Go see your mama. She misses you. Moms are like that."

Catherine squealed and ran over to Aurora and Ruby, tears pooling as she rubbed their cheeks. She couldn't stop touching their soft fur, reassuring herself they were actually there.

"Are they okay? Did he hurt them?" She scanned them for injury.

"I don't think so. They were in the backseat."

She rolled onto her back and let her fur babies crawl over her. They meowed and purred.

"I'm so sorry you went through that." She stroked their fur. "Angelo, can you get them some treats, please?"

When she glanced at him, he was already holding the container. "I know the deal around here," he said with a grin. He shook it, and the kittens darted in his direction, rubbing against his legs as if they were laced with catnip. More than ever, she had the sense of how natural he seemed in her place. Like he belonged here.

With her.

ANGELO

Once the police finally left, Angelo sat with Cate in her living room. What a long day.

They each had glasses of hot chocolate with peppermint schnapps. She rested her head on his shoulder. This was what he wanted. A perfect, still moment like this.

If he didn't take a chance now, he'd regret it. Every moment in the future when he would spend time sweating in some arid sandpit, or be freezing in some mountain cave, would be a reminder of what he could have had if he'd had the balls to say it, and it would hammer away in his mind.

If she went for it.

He took a sip of the cocoa and placed it on a coaster. "Cate, I've been thinking."

She pulled her head from his shoulder and gazed at him. "About what?"

"My life, basically." Oh hell, this was it. Heat pulsed through his veins. He peeled off the emotional armor.

"In what way?"

As she gazed at him with such warmth and understanding, he found answers to questions he didn't know he had. She made it all worth it. It didn't make logical sense, but did it have to?

Fuck it. No regrets. He manned up.

"You know it's been a tough year."

She sighed. "Yes. I'm sorry."

"I'm not fishing for sympathy but trying to be honest with you. Military men have a rep for being crap at revealing feelings."

Her patient expression allowed him to confide on his own timeline. For that he was grateful.

"A SEAL should know when they have to exit the game," he added. "It's what's best for the team. If I'm not sharp, I can hold them back."

She furrowed her brows. "You were incredible tonight. I was so blind about the situation. You were the one who saw things clearly. The only one. You saved my life, and potentially others as well. The way you figured out how to deal with the situation." She let out a low whoosh. "If that's not being sharp and resourceful, I don't know what is."

He swallowed a lump that swelled in his throat, threatening to capture his voice. Her belief in him meant so much, crumbling his uncertainty that he was too damaged.

"What I'm saying is that there's one thing clear in all the uncertainty about my future. I want you in it."

She covered her heart and sighed.

"I don't know what I want to do five years from now or even five months. But I know I want to be with you. However you'll have me. *If* you'll have me."

She watched him with wide eyes, and lips parted.

"It meant everything that you called me today. You trusted me. And I always want to be the man who's there for you. I've never been so scared than in that moment when I saw you tied up. Not even in battle. It affected me so intensely, so personal, because it is."

He took a moment and caressed her cheek. "I want us to be together. Every day. If that's not possible, once a month, once every six months—as long as I know I'll be with you again, that's enough for me."

"Oh..." Her eyes glistened. "I don't know how to respond."

This was it. Time to lay it all out. And if he ended up getting shot down with verbal bullets, well, so be it.

"Say you'll give us a chance?"

She searched his eyes for what seemed like decades before a grin spread across her face. "Yes."

Angelo jumped to his feet and took her by the hands, bringing her to stand. He lifted her and spun her in a circle while he hollered in jubilance. "You won't regret it, Cate. I'll strive every day to be the man you deserve."

She tilted her head. "You already are much more than that to me." She gazed up at him with a heartfelt warmth in her eyes. "Don't you know, Angelo?"

"Know what?"

"You've always been the one who truly sees me. Who appreciates me, quirks and all." She covered his cheek. "You've always been the one."

EPILOGUE

CATHERINE

The bridesmaids walked down the grassy path decorated on either side with baby's breath. Catherine's palms turned clammy. She was next. Nerves spiraled, just like last year at Diana's wedding. Only this time Catherine was the bride.

All eyes on her. No escape.

Yes, she could back up. Run from the spotlight. She wouldn't be the first runaway bride.

Focus. Think of a happy memory.

Angelo had proposed four months ago. She let the memory of their stroll along Cliff Walk calm her. He'd surprised her as the sun set when he bent down to one knee and pulled out a black box.

"Cate, coming home to you brings me more happiness than I ever imagined. I love you and want to be with you always. Will you marry me?" With a lopsided grin, he added, "Please don't make me have to propose three times like my Dad."

She'd laughed through tears of joy and then quoted his mother. "Yes, you crazy fool. Now shut up and kiss me."

He'd laughed. "You're going to fit in perfectly as a DeMarchis."

As the ecstasy drifted and reality set in, she furrowed her brows. All that attention on her as a bride? She cringed. "Can we elope?"

"Why?" When she'd squirmed, Angelo squeezed her arm. "I know you hate the attention on you, but can you think about it? I want us to have this moment. Share it with our family and friends. And my team. They're like brothers to me. Besides, I can't imagine the uproar in my house if I tell my mom that I'm getting married and she can't be part of it." He chuckled. "She'd kill me. Kill me twice, if she could."

Catherine had smiled. "Okay, okay. We won't elope. I prefer a live husband on my wedding night. My family would give me hell, too. But it has to be a small wedding—not one of those massive affairs."

"Deal." He'd sealed it with a kiss. A long, deep, passionate kiss, like the ones she received when he came home to her. That was one of the perks of him going away. The reunions were never bland. Sure, the separations were difficult, but they were figuring out how to make their relationship work.

"Are you ready?" Her father brought her back to the present.

It was her turn. She released a slow exhale and held his arm. "Yes."

As they took the first few steps, her heartbeat soared. Everyone was staring at her. She flushed. What if she tripped and fell on her face? What if she froze up when she had to repeat the vows? What if her anxiety grew so high that she fainted?

She used her soothing technique with counting, but even that didn't calm her racing heartbeat. She clung onto her father's arm.

Remember what Angelo told you. Right, he said to forget about everyone else there and just look for him.

She glanced down the aisle. He stood waiting for her, looking incredible in a tux. A strong, steady anchor braced before the bay.

The flowers, the ocean, the people who all surrounded her disappeared. All she saw was him. Angelo DeMarchis, the one man she'd never forgotten, was going to be her husband. The one man who she measured everyone else up to in comparison would be her partner in life.

Her galloping pulse leveled out. The anxiety slowly dissipated. This was a happy day, the best one of her life. Better than any moment of academic or career success.

Catherine beamed and strode toward her fiancé, never feeling more confident about the future.

ANGELO

Angelo sucked in a breath when Cate walked toward him. His heart pounded like the steady staccato of a machine gun. Shit, she was right. This was terrifying. Why did they invite an audience in on the biggest step in their lives?

Breathe. He inhaled the scent of the ocean behind him, using the SEAL breathing technique to soothe his rising anxiety, ignoring the muffled chuckle of his brothers beside him.

"You're just getting married, not performing brain surgery," Matty had said minutes ago upon witnessing Angelo's restlessness with being unable to stand still.

A stifling heat warmed his skin far more than the setting sun burning down on him, making his tux feel as oppressive as if wearing body armor.

Were they making a mistake? Sure, she'd been handling his assignments well. He'd moved stateside six months ago for a new billet training junior corpsmen. Instead of being overseas for much of the year, he was closer to Cate. Closer to his heart.

Still, they were living in different states on the east coast as she still taught at the university and he finished out his final tour before moving in with her and the cats in Providence. The distance made their reunions combustible enough to blow up a lab. But what if she eventually thought that the baggage that came with being a military wife wasn't worth it? She wouldn't be the first person to decide they were unsuited for the lifestyle. And what if someone like that Trent guy endangered her life? Even if that guy was receiving psychiatric care somewhere after fixating on Cate, that didn't mean he or someone else couldn't get to her. And what if Angelo wasn't around to help?

He took in a deep breath and glanced at a few married guys from his team. He then glanced over at his parents. His mother was already crying, tears of joy running down her face. His father held his chin high with a proud, happy expression. They all had faith in each other, their marriage, and didn't let the hard times tear them apart. Angelo could do that. He'd never stray from Cate. Why would he? She was the most amazing woman he'd ever met. No one compared. There was no one like her.

He had to have faith in her. Faith in them.

He caught her eye. She smiled—a beautiful wondrous smile that sent all his fears flying.

They'd make it. He had no doubt. He trusted her with his whole heart. What he felt for her was stronger than any separation. They'd built a foundation ten years ago. Back when he knew he'd met someone special, but he was too young to know she was the one—the only one—for him.

Picturing one of her recent emails, he smiled. She'd sent him photos of her in different bikinis asking him to choose his favorite for their honeymoon to Bermuda. He picked them all. They had plenty of days sailing in Newport in their future.

He was looking forward to the next ten years with Cate. Hell, the next fifty.

She was moving closer now, just steps away. Her eyes shone with excitement, bright and hopeful. They said that weddings were for the bride, but damn, he'd never forget this moment. His mind zoomed with images of their future. Christmases with presents stuffed under the tree. Taking their kids along a holiday stroll in Newport and watching their awe at the lights.

Kids? Yes, kids. He was ready to start a family with her soon. He pictured her belly round with his child. She'd be a terrific mother. He hoped their kids were smart and beautiful as she was.

He suppressed a laugh. For a hardened SEAL who swore he had no room in his world for a wife and kids, he'd softened like a well-loved teddy bear. All the uncertainties in his confused state of mind had begun to vanish. He knew what he wanted—a life with Cate—wherever that brought them.

Her father kissed her on the cheek and then took his seat. Angelo took Cate's hand. The familiar bolt of heat zipped through him. She gazed at him with such warmth in her eyes. Her smile turned luminous. It turned his insides as mushy as grits, as Matty had described. Hell, Angelo had never felt so warm and squishy.

Ready to take the next step in his life, with Cate by his side, the remaining anxiety lifted. Damn, he was ready to take on a tank.

Tonight, he'd show her how much he appreciated her taking this leap. He'd spend their wedding night making sure it was one she'd always remember.

He stepped closer to her, and her eyes sparkled with a knowing glint, as if she knew exactly what was on his mind. If not, he'd make sure she did tonight.

"Dearly beloved, we are gathered here today…"

Angelo winked at Cate. They had this.

EPILOGUE 2 - A SNEAK PEEK WITH VINCE

VINCE

"*Til* death do you part? That is one messed up mission." Vince gave his older brother Angelo, a lopsided smile.

They stood before Narragansett Bay where Angelo had just married his fiancée Catherine in an outdoor ceremony. An occasional sea breeze rolled in with its heady fragrance, cooling the heat of the summer day. The sun had begun to set, painting fiery streaks across the sky.

"And he volunteered for it, no less," Vince's younger brother, Matty, added.

They all wore matching tuxedos with blue cummerbunds. Angelo and Matty had trimmed their hair and beards for the wedding, while Vince had his Marine-required clean-shaven face and close haircut.

"It's a marriage, not a mission." Angelo laughed. "When you find the right woman, you go for it." He nodded as if it was a solid declaration.

Vince and Matty exchanged a skeptical glance.

"That explains why it took you two over a decade to get hitched," Vince quipped.

Angelo grunted and smiled. "You know what I mean. We were kids back then. Our lives went in separate directions."

"Just giving you a hard time." Vince patted Angelo on the back. "Congrats, man. I'm happy for you."

His mother walked towards them with arms raised for a hug and smiling, although her eyes were glossy. Her dark hair was coiled without a hair out of place and she wore a blue dress with several silky layers. "Here comes Ma."

Matty covered his mouth and whispered, "Mother-of-the-Groom-Zilla."

Vince knew what was coming next. Since Angelo had announced he was getting married, their mother had been relentless. His engagement instigated many questions about when Vince and Matty would settle down.

"My eldest married!" She wrapped her arms around Angelo, and then attempted to pull Vince and Matty into the hug as well. They both leaned in to the awkward embrace with their mom as she tried to hug the three grown men.

"I never thought I'd see the day! What with you boys deployed here and there and it being almost impossible to get you all in Newport at the same time." She pulled back and moved her hard-stare along the three of them like a drill sergeant. "Family is the most important thing."

Vince had been reminded of that many times, but he didn't blame his mother for repeating it. She was the one who was responsible for keeping their family together while their father had been out to sea, which had happened many times during his career in the navy. It couldn't have been easy raising three raucous boys largely by herself.

"When am I going to see the two of you getting married?" Her eyes traveled from Vince to Matty.

Damn, that was quick.

"To each other?" Matty teased. "We're brothers! That's not really legal, Ma. Besides, Vince is too pretty for my taste."

She swatted Matty's arm. "You know what I mean. Everything's a joke with you. One day, you'll meet the right woman, and then you'll start to take life more seriously."

"Until then, I'll live the dream." He cocked his head and stared out to the sea with a carefree expression.

She pulled her gaze to Vince, waiting.

"Not going to happen while I'm in the Marines, Ma." He shook his head and glanced out to the other attendees, focusing on his cousins, Jack and Antonio, from Boston, who were also Marines. He'd catch up with them more later, but for now, he had to escape the pressure to settle down. He deflected the attention to Angelo. "Now that Angelo's married, maybe you'll have grandbabies soon."

She clutched her hands. "I've been waiting to be a grandmother for so long!"

Angelo shot Vince a *you're-gonna-get-it* look.

While she refocused on Angelo, Vince stole the opportunity to escape as she could be more tenacious than a devil dog when it came to her sons.

Matty's voice trailed after Vince. "Aaand Vince disappears with his classic Irish goodbye."

Vince acknowledged them with a wave, but didn't turn back. He needed some space. He slipped inside the venue, an elegant stone seaside venue on the ocean. A woman with honey-brown hair pulled into a bun caught his attention. A strand fell across her cheek. She wore black slacks and a white blouse and carried a tray of cupcakes. He caught her gaze, and sucked in a breath.

Seconds passed and neither spoke. His heart hammered in his chest. He should say something, but he continued to stare into her large brown eyes.

Where did all the oxygen go?

Her full pink lips parted as if she was about to speak, but then she tore her gaze away and shook her head as if confused by her reaction. He blinked and inhaled, just as taken off-guard by his response. So what if she was hot? It wasn't as if he'd never seen a pretty woman before.

Still, he tracked where she walked. She headed toward the main room where the reception was being held. Guests were tearing it up on the dance floor to *Uptown Funk*. No way would he join in. He didn't get the appeal of flailing arms and legs like an idiot in front of an audience.

The ring bearer ran in the pretty brunette's path, followed by the flower girl.

"Watch out," Vince warned, rushing over.

It was too late. She tripped over the kids and headed for the floor.

He managed to reach her before the cupcakes crashed onto the tiled floor.

Some of the cupcakes fell off the tray, frosting first. Yet, they'd salvaged the tray, at least for the most part.

"Are you okay?" He placed the tray on a nearby table.

She blinked a few times and her lips parted. "Yes. I didn't even see them coming."

His jaw tightened. Had he distracted her with his idiot stare? "They came out of nowhere."

She glanced at the tray and straightened the toppled cupcakes. "Crap."

"You're down a few troops, but I think they can be salvaged." He picked up a couple of cupcakes and placed them upright.

She gazed at him as if perplexed and then shook her head. "Thanks." She brushed the hair out of her face, but managed to smear white frosting on her cheek.

A chuckle burst out of him without warning as the ridiculousness of the situation caught up. Here he was in a monkey suit at his brother's wedding with a beautiful woman and fallen cupcakes.

"What's so funny?" Her brows furrowed.

He reached out and wiped some frosting off her cheek, displaying it on his finger tip. "Just a little frosting."

"Oh!" Her cheeks turned pink against the white frosting. "I'm a hot mess."

ANGELO

He chuckled. "Hot, yes. But not a mess."

"Thanks, I guess." She picked up one of the cupcakes off the floor. With a wry grin, she asked, "Have a sweet tooth?" She raised the cupcake toward his cheek as if ready to smear him with frosting.

He stopped laughing and waved his hands in surrender. "No, I can't mess up this tux. It's a rental I have to return tomorrow."

"Fine." She conceded with a tilt of her head and a sassy grin. "But, only because you helped me avoid a catastrophe."

"At a wedding no less, that's colossal confectionery carnage."

"That's quite the alliteration over a cupcake collision." Her eyes twinkled and her lips curled into a demi-smile.

Wordplay? Hell yes. Nothing hotter than verbal foreplay. How could he keep them talking?

Ah, he'd be a gentleman and offer to help. He rose and lifted the tray from the table. "Where can I bring these?"

She stood, wiping the frosting from her cheek onto her apron. "You don't have to do that. It's what I'm here for."

"Not a problem. I'm the best man. I can at least do something more useful than standing around in this penguin suit."

"Okay then. This way." She led him to a table where a white three-tier wedding cake stood. "We'll put the cupcakes on either side of the cake."

He stared at the selection. "Cake and cupcakes? I've already been hit with a sugar rush."

"*Everybody* loves cupcakes. Trust me, they'll likely be all gone while the cake will remain barely touched."

He shrugged. "You're the expert."

While she went to the kitchen, he debated his next move. Would it be wrong to hit on the caterer at his brother's wedding?

When she returned, he said, "I'm Vince. I apologize for my family and friends in advance. An Italian and Armenian family and a Navy crew. Who will be the loudest and most boisterous is a tough call."

"No problem." She grinned. "I'm Emma. This isn't my first wedding. I think I've seen it all."

Might as well hone in. "To make up for a loud night and messy cleanup ahead, how about I take you out tomorrow, Emma?"

Maybe not the slickest segue, but it was out there.

She eyed him, studying his face. In the few seconds that followed, his pulse quickened.

"Sorry, but I don't date military."

Damn. Shot down. Still, he wasn't ready to retreat yet. "How do you know I'm military?"

"Your haircut announces it like a billboard in Times Square. And like you said, a Navy crew is here tonight."

True. Although he'd let it grow out a bit before the wedding, the signature high-and-tight style still gave him away. "Not Navy." He took smug satisfaction in announcing that separation, just as he and his brothers had ribbed each other a thousand times. "Marine."

"Even worse!" She snorted. "Do I need to get an extra place setting for your ego?" she added with a flirtatious smile.

"No, I left it on base while I'm on leave." He stepped closer to her. "Which means I'm alone and could use some company."

She arched her brow. "Your family will be happy to accommodate that request, I'm sure." She turned with her tray of cupcakes and walked away from him.

Screw it, he manned up and gave it another shot. "I'd much rather talk to you, Emma. What time are you done here?"

She turned over her shoulder and gazed at him with an amused expression. "Around midnight."

"Meet me for a drink." He made a point of making a statement, not asking a question.

She appraised him with a lingering glance. "A drink?"

"Right. Not a date, just a drink. You can't leave me hanging on the night of my brother's wedding, can you?" he cocked his head and shrugged with mock innocence.

She bit her lip. "I'll think about it."

It wasn't a no. With the appreciative glimmer in her eyes, he'd put his money on yes.

"Until the witching hour." He gave her a half bow and turned away. Confidence was critical for any victory.

More alliteration. Amusement tugged at his lips. If luck was on his side, he'd have an unforgettable night with Emma, the cupcake caterer.

READ WHAT HAPPENS NEXT!

Read Vince's story now!

Binge the entire Anchor Me series.

BE A VIP READER!

Join my Facebook reader group!

Visit lisacarlislebooks.com for the latest releases, news, book trailers, and more!

Sign up for my newsletter. New readers receive a welcome gift, exclusive bonus content, and more, including Antonio's story.

Download Antonio: A Second Chance Marine Romance for free today!

BOOK LIST

Anchor Me

Meet the DeMarchis brothers and their family in these romances featuring Navy SEALs or Marines!

- *Antonio (a novella available for free for subscribers. Sign up at lisacarlislebooks.com)*
- *Angelo*
- *Vince*
- *Matty*
- *Jack*
- *Slade*
- *Mark*

Night Eagle Operations

Military romantic suspense with a supernatural twist

When Darkness Whispers

Salem Supernaturals, Underground Encounters, and the White Mountain Shifters, are connected series. You can start with any of them and do not have to read in any order.

Salem Supernaturals

A witch without magic inherits a house with quirky roommates, and magical sparks fly!

- *Rebel Spell*
- *Hot in Witch City*
- *Dancing with My Elf*

White Mountain Shifters (Howls Romance)

Fated mates and forbidden love. When wolf shifters find their fated mate, the trouble is only just beginning.

- *The Reluctant Wolf and His Fated Mate*
- *The Wolf and His Forbidden Witch*
- *The Alpha and His Enemy Wolf*

Underground Encounters

Steamy paranormal romances set in an underground goth club that attracts vampires, witches, shifters, and gargoyles.

- *Book 0: CURSED (a gargoyle shifter story)*
- *Book 1: SMOLDER (a vampire / firefighter romance)*
- *Book 2: FIRE (a witch / firefighter romance)*
- *Book 3: IGNITE (a feline shifter / rock star romance)*
- *Book 4: BURN (a vampire / shapeshifter rock romance)*
- *Book 5: HEAT (a gargoyle shifter romance)*
- *Book 6: BLAZE (a gargoyle shifter rockstar romance)*
- *Book 7: COMBUST (vampire / witch romances)*
- *Book 8: INFLAME (a gargoyle shifter / witch romance)*
- *Book 9: TORCH (a gargoyle shifter / werewolf romance*
- *Book 10: SCORCH (an incubus vs succubus demon romance)*

Chateau Seductions

An art colony on a remote New England island lures creative types—and supernatural characters. Steamy paranormal romances.

- *Darkness Rising*
- *Dark Velvet*
- *Dark Muse*
- *Dark Stranger*
- *Dark Pursuit*

Highland Gargoyle

Gargoyle shifters, wolf shifters, and tree witches have divided the Isle of Stone after a great battle 25 years ago. One risk changes it all…

- *Knights of Stone: Mason*
- *Knights of Stone: Lachlan*
- *Knights of Stone: Bryce*
- *Seth: a wolf shifter romance in the series*
- *Knights of Stone: Calum*
- *Knights of Stone: Gavin (coming soon)*

Stone Sentries

Meet your perfect match the night of the super moon — or your perfect match for the night. A cop teams up with a gargoyle shifter when demons attack Boston.

- *Tempted by the Gargoyle*
- *Enticed by the Gargoyle*
- *Captivated by the Gargoyle*

Berkano Vampires

A shared author world with dystopian paranormal romances.

- *Immortal Resistance*

Blood Courtesans

A shared author world with the vampire blood courtesans.

- *Pursued: Mia*

Visit LisaCarlisleBooks.com to learn more and to subscribe to my reader newsletter!

Don't miss any new releases!

Follow Me on Amazon

Follow Me on Bookbub

ACKNOWLEDGMENTS

As always, I am so grateful to everyone who helps make each book possible, helping me shape the ideas in my head into a story. Huge thanks to my critique partners, editors, beta readers, ARC readers, Street Team, and you, the reader! Thank you for spending time with me with characters I love.

ABOUT THE AUTHOR

USA Today bestselling author Lisa Carlisle loves to write stories about wounded or misunderstood heroes finding their happily ever after. They often face the temptation of fated and forbidden love--so difficult to resist!

Her romances have been named Top Picks at Night Owl Reviews and the Romance Reviews.

She draws on her travels and experiences in her stories, which include deploying to Okinawa, Japan, while in the Marines, backpacking alone through Europe, and living in Paris before returning to the U.S. She owned a bookstore for a few years as she loves to read. She's now married to a fantastic man, and they have two kids, two cats, and too many fish.

Visit her website for more on books, trailers, playlists, and more:

Lisacarlislebooks.com

Sign up for her newsletter to hear about new releases, specials, and freebies:

http://www.lisacarlislebooks.com/subscribe/

Lisa loves to connect with readers. You can find her on:

Facebook

Twitter

Pinterest

Instagram

Goodreads